Happy Hour

Happy Hour

Gina M. DeLuca

Writers Club Press
San Jose New York Lincoln Shanghai

Happy Hour

Writers Club Press
an imprint of iUniverse.com, Inc.

For information address:
iUniverse.com, Inc.
5220 S 16th, Ste. 200
Lincoln, NE 68512
www.iuniverse.com

ISBN: 0-595-17848-0

Printed in the United States of America

*Many thanks to my friends and family who have supported
and encouraged me throughout my first book ordeal*

Follow your dreams

CHAPTER ONE

It was raining as usual in South Florida on a muggy Friday afternoon in August. Mayla was staring out of her office window from the tenth floor that over looks popular Las Olas Boulevard. She let out a slight sigh as she thought of how she would make it home in the traffic, with the rain on a Friday afternoon.

"Maybe I'll work late." She mumbled to herself. She puts her head back down to study her computer. Mayla was a legal secretary for a prestigious law firm in downtown Ft. Lauderdale. She did not seem to mind the same daily routine of nine to five. She was comfortable in her condo that was handed down to her from her fragile white haired grandmother who passed away two years ago. It was an older condo but she loved it because it sat off A1A, the road that ran north and south along the beach. In the mornings she was greeted by vibrant orange sunrises and at night she could watch the seagulls fish for dinner all while she sat on her balcony enjoying the smell of the salty air that the summer breeze had brought her. It was a two-bedroom condo with a small kitchen and a large living area. She is looking into having it renovated to give it a formal dining room that will have an ocean front view and a larger island kitchen. Mayla loves to cook and entertain so much that some of her friends would ask her to cater special dinners for them.

"Mayla," a head peeked around the corner into her office, "We are going to happy hour tonight. Want to join us?"

It was Shelby. Her blond hair dangled around her face as she spoke. She was the obnoxious one in the firm who always spoke what was on her mind. She was entertaining and could always give every one near her a good laugh.

"Sure. What time and where?" Mayla replied as she took her eyes off of her computer and looked up.

"Five at Riverfront. I'll come get you."

Shelby ran off to her corner of the office.

Mayla Ann Martin was single in her late twenty's. The brown haired blue eyed girl was a native Floridian, something you don't hear too much of. Most Florida residents are from the East Coast such as New York or New Jersey.

Five o'clock. Time for happy hour. Shelby dragged Mayla from her office and joined the others in the elevator on their way down to Riverfront. Tom Wheeler, a successful partner at the law firm grinned from ear to ear when he saw Mayla get on the elevator. He has been trying unsuccessfully to get her into bed for more than two years now.

"What are your plans for the weekend Mayla? Do they include me?"

"Not unless you can get out of that tacky Guido suit of yours and get your hands dirty in my kitchen." Mayla replied sarcastically knowing that Tom has never done a stitch of hard labor in his life.

"Oh an invitation! Do you want me to cook for you?"

"What would we have? Hotdogs?" She turned her back towards him.

"What is a hotdog mademoiselle?" He faked his French accent.

Tom was a player. He was mostly all talk and no action. He rarely had a date and if he did he would never get a second one. He tried to hard to impress people. It was difficult to understand why he was like this. He was a partner in the firm and he was very handsome with his dark hair and brown eyes. Perhaps he was picked on in is early childhood years. At least that was the conclusion that Mayla had come to.

The elevator doors opened and one by one the lawyers, secretaries and office personnel walked out. The rain had come to a slight drizzle and was bearable enough to walk through to happy hour. The bar was not as crowded as usual.

"The rain must have scared everyone off." Shelby said with disappointment, "No chance of finding a boy to play with tonight!"

"Why don't you try to control those hormones Shelby." Tom chewed on his cocktail straw. "If you did, someone may actually find you attractive instead of a blond bimbo."

Shelby moved herself close to Tom's face. "Go to hell Tom! You should talk. You always have your tongue down someone's throat! Trying to impress your coworkers, that's very attractive!"

"It would be nice if you two would stop just once at happy hour!" Mayla exclaimed as she intercepted the conversation, "You are both little horny people and should spend the weekend in bed fucking! You're the perfect couple!"

"No, I don't think Tom's penis is big enough for me."

"That's because you're so worn out."

Mayla rolled her eyes and walked away from the two. "Those two are made for each other."

"Hi Michael." Mayla said as she propped herself on a barstool next to him, "Buying me a drink?"

"Sure. What is your pleasure?"

"I can't tell you that Michael, but I'll have a vodka martini."

The firm Mayla worked for were mostly outgoing young professionals.

"Have big plans for the weekend Mayla?"

"I'm remodeling my kitchen and have to meet with the contractor. They had a problem getting a building permit. Work can only be done from nine to five Monday through Friday. I have a bunch of blue hairs in my building. They would complain if I hung a picture after five. How about you?"

"Marlene and I are taking the kids to Orlando. We need to get away and have some fun."

"Sounds like fun Michael."

"Yep."

The bartender placed the martinis in front of them. Mayla picked hers up and said, "Cheers!"

Michael nodded and smiled as he lifted his glass to hers.

Michael Devon was the senior partner in the law firm. He was always the serious one in the group. It must be because he has a wife and two daughters. His wife Marlene was a stay at home mom who took care of the two girls Samantha, six and Tallie, four. Michael's family seemed to be his main focus in life. They had a large home out in the Weston area. A growing family community not more than seven years old. It boasts the Weston Hills golf and country club, a few restaurants and newer grocery stores. Sometimes the firm would have golf outings at Michael's club on Wednesdays to break up the week. Most of the attorneys were avid golfers. A requirement living in South Florida.

"You seem down Michael. What's up?"

"Just a tough week."

"Well, you'll have a great weekend."

"I think so."

Mayla turned her head to look around the bar and see if there was anyone interesting that she might like to talk too. Tom and Shelby were in the corner having a sleazy conversation about sex. A few of the other legal secretaries were bitching about their salaries and the mailroom boys were trying to pick up two unsuspecting dumb girls wearing shorts skirts and bellybutton rings. They were in their early twenties.

"We work at Max, Devon and Wheeler."

Mayla studied the boys and their tactics. The girls would coo and blush as the boys talked to them. The girls must have thought they scored big with these two. They were already exchanging numbers. The two girls left looking behind them as they walked out the door smiling at the horny mailroom boys. Jimmy and Kenny looked at each other and said, "Next!" Hungry little bastards. Her happy hour hangout was nothing but a meat market.

"I wonder if I ever acted that silly?" Mayla asked.

"How silly?" Asked Michael.

"Oh Michael, look these people. They do anything, say anything, just for a number."

"We've all been there Mayla." He plucked his olive Off the end of the cellophane stick.

"I don't believe I've ever behaved like that." Mayla insisted.

"I know you have."

"When did I ever act like that?" Mayla asked in disbelief. "I have never! I am certain!"

"Just last week." Michael said with a smirk as he took a sip of his martini. "Ah let's see, his name was,"

"Oh please Michael! John and I are just good friends! I have known him since I have been working for this firm."

"Yep."

"Michael you're not being fair."

"About what?"

"It was strictly business."

"Then why did your eyes light up when he told you he was divorced last week?"

"They did not!"

"You are an easy book to read Miss Mayla Martin."

"Whatever Michael. So can you put in a good word?"

Michael smiled as he took his last sip if his martini, "I'll see what I can do."

"Are you leaving?"

"Yes, we have an early start."

"Have a great time! See you Monday."

Mayla watched as Michael left the bar. Something just didn't seem right with him. He seemed stressed. Mayla removed herself from the noise of the crowd and began to people watch. She found people watching more entertaining than the movies. Studying their moves. Watching the two women in the corner was her most interesting find of the night. One would talk about her divorce and the other spoke of her affair with her married boss. The blond woman lectured her friend. "Leave him. He's a married man, and he's your boss."

"I don't care. He has money and I don't. If he tries to fire me. I'll cry sexual harassment."

"You have no spine." They carried on with their argument for quite sometime.

Nearly thirty minutes had passed before Shelby interrupted her.

"Are you there? Hello? Earth to Mayla."

Mayla turned to look at Shelby.

"I'm here and I'm leaving. Call me this weekend if you want to go biking." She faced back towards the bar placing her empty martini glass on the tiled counter top.

Mayla knew Shelby would never call because she doesn't have an athletic muscle in her body. Mayla removed herself from her co-workers and the barflies that were searching for a one-night stand. It was seven-thirty already and she wanted to run some errands before the stores closed. She walked back to the parking garage in the damp air. The garage was attached to her office. She took the elevator to the third floor where the parking spaces were clearly marked "Max, Devon.", as Wheeler would not fit. Mayla maneuvered her key in her BMW when she looked up and saw Michael putting his brief case and a box in his car.

"I thought you left?"

"I did. I had to come back to the office. I forgot some documents for a client of mine in Orlando. I thought I'd drop them off since I was going to be there."

"Well have a good time!"

Mayla got in her car and sped off.

The rest of the office stayed at happy hour that night until nearly midnight. Jimmy and Ken, the mailroom boys successfully picked up several different girls. On Monday they would post their numbers they collected on the bulletin board in the mailroom. Each week they would try to set a record for numbers collected.

That night after Mayla and Michael left, Shelby met a handsome man eleven years her senior. His name is Robert. A tall man with salt and pepper hair. He owns a prestigious brokerage firm in Hollywood.

"You have very beautiful eyes."

Shelby blushed with a smile and simply said, "Thank you."

"Can I buy you a drink?"

"Sure. Absolute cranberry please."

"Right away." Robert called the bartender.

"Is this your happy hour hang out?"

"I guess you could say that." The bartender gave her the vodka cranberry. She thanked him then turned to Robert, "And thank you."

"I'm Robert Edwards." He extended his hand.

"Shelby Peterson. Nice to meet you."

"I'm trying to pick you up. How am I doing?"

"I'd say good but your initial pick-up line of 'you have beautiful eyes' is a bit hokey." She sipped her drink.

"I guess it is." Robert blushed. "Where do you work?"

"I'm a legal secretary at Max, Devon and Wheeler. Have you heard of us?"

"Can't say I have. Are these some of the people you work with?"

"Yes. A few."

"Are you married?" Robert asked as he picked up her hand.

"No." She sighed.

"I find it hard to believe no one has your heart."

"I guess I haven't found him yet."

"Well, he will be a very lucky man. Very lucky. I hope I have a shot at it."

Robert mesmerized Shelby. He seemed so confident in a charming yet in an unsure way.

"I hope he calls, I could use a date."

"May I call you?" Robert asked.

Bingo! Thank you!

"I would be disappointed if you didn't."

Shelby reached for her pocket book where she took out her business card and handed it to Robert.

"I'll call."

Robert tucked the business card in his suit then reached for his pant pocket where he pulled out a gold money clip filled with hundred dollars bills. He peeled one off handed it to the bartender and casually told him, "Please, keep the change. I've had a wonderful evening."

Shelby was in awe over his candidness. Shelby watched as Robert walked out the open door. He handed his ticket to the valet where in exchange he gave him a shiny black Ferrari spider.

Holy cows. A Ferrari.

Shelby left shortly after Robert.

Tom was the last to leave happy hour. He drank more than he should have. He had to take a taxi home.

"I'm going to pay for this tomorrow." He mumbled as he sat in the back of big yellow cab that departed from the curb.

CHAPTER TWO

Saturday morning came in a hurry as Mayla hopped out of bed.

"Oh my god the contractor is going to be here any second! I haven't showered, haven't had coffee,…"

The doorbell rang.

"Shit! Shit! Shit!" She was running to wash her face and get dressed, "Just a minute! Coming!"

She gathered herself as she unlocked the front door, "I'm sorry, I've overslept!"

Mayla opened the door to find the burly contractor standing there.

"Miss Martin, nice to see you again." He extended his hand to shake hers as he walked into her condo. "This is going to take about two weeks. Do you have the original blue prints and the architects drawings?"

The burly man stayed for a half an hour looking around the condo taking last minute notes.

"We'll see you Monday!" He smiled as he closed the door behind him.

"Ok Vermin!" she looked at her parakeet and said, "Mommy has many errands to run today! You be a good boy and maybe when I come home I will let you out of your cage."

Mayla blew her bird a kiss goodbye. She got the name Vermin from her girlfriend's son. He was with her when she bought him.

Mayla's first stop was the home improvement store. She was there to pick out paint samples for her home. She found herself under a bright light staring at several different shades of yellows and khakis not realizing there were so many to chose from.

Choose a color Miss Martin. Any color will do. She pretended to be interrogated. As she turned away to focus her eyes on something else, she spotted a familiar face.

"Hi Mayla!" It was Michael's wife. "Michael said you were remodeling your condo, how is it coming along?"

"They start on Monday. They haven't even started and I can't wait until it's done." Replied Mayla, "What are you doing here?"

"Well since Michael went to New York for business I thought I could catch up on some gardening." She pointed to her cart filled with colorful flowers.

"I see. I'm trying to pick colors for my house. I thought I had a good idea of what I wanted until I got here. There's so much to choose from."

"There sure is. It took me forever to decide on the color of the guest bath. Well have fun. I got to run, the girls are at my mother's and she has company coming."

"See you."

Mayla turned in disbelief. *Could Michael be having an affair? Why would he tell me he was going to Orlando with his wife? I can't imagine Michael with another woman! Marlene and those girls are his life!*

Mayla's cell phone rang and disrupted her thoughts.

"Hello?"

"Hey Mayla, its Shelby. Guess what?"

"What?"

"I met a man!"

"When last night?" Mayla flipped through color swatches as she spoke to Shelby.

"Yes, after you left. His name is Robert. He seems to be successful and he owns a brokerage firm in Hollywood. He is very handsome! His hair is salt and pepper! What a turn on! I, I should settle down or I may have an orgasm just talking about him!"

"Good lord get a hold of yourself. When are you going out?"

"Well he has to call first."

"I supposed that would be a good start. What else can you tell me?"

"He drives a Ferrari! He's forty-five."

"A Ferrari? *Wow!*"

"I've never been in one!"

"Well looks like you will have your chance. Are you sure that he's not too old for you?"

"No. If he calls, I'm going. Besides, I have no one else knocking on my door."

"Well, that's true."

"Hey girl, that wasn't very nice!"

"You said it!"

"Movie tonight?" asked Shelby.

"Sure."

Mayla finished running her errands long enough for her to get home and take a nap before the movie.

"Ring, ring, ring." The phone awoke Mayla from her deep sleep.

"Hello?"

"Mayla, it's Tom. What are you doing tonight?"

"Well Tom, I've already decided I'm not going on a date with you."

"I know that. I am, well I don't have any plans and was wondering…"

"Shelby and I are going to catch a movie." She intercepted the conversation. "You're more than welcome to come. But don't try to hold my hand!"

"I won't." He pouted.

Shelby, Tom and Mayla met at the big theater on US1 in Pompano Beach. Neon lights lit the outside of the theater.

"Anybody sneak some snacks?"

"No Tom," replied Shelby, "You make the big bucks, go get us some popcorn!"

After the sci-fi movie the three moved to a late night diner down the road.

"Hey," asked Mayla, "Does anyone know what's up with Michael? He seemed to be in an odd frame of mind at happy hour."

"I haven't noticed anything, but then again, I've been so wrapped up in the Riley case I haven't noticed." Tom said as he bit into a sandwich.

"How is that case going? Have they found any more evidence against Mr. Riley?" asked Shelby.

"I hope not. This guy is going to do enough time the way it is."

"Insurance fraud. I swear everyone is trying to make an easy buck. It seems like the thing to do is to come up with some type of scam and that is how you become filthy rich. Everyone wants a free ride." Said Mayla, "and my taxes get to pay for it."

"So Tom," asked Shelby, "Did you pick anyone up last night?"

"No but I saw the old guy you were hanging with. He looks old enough to be your father."

"He's only eleven years older."

"Drives a Ferrari too. That's right up your alley Shelby."

"Jealous?"

"Of what? His age? I don't think so."

"Here we go again." Mayla mumbled as she stuffed a French fry in her mouth.

The three finished their late night snack and headed home.

Monday morning came all too soon for Mayla. She had not finished moving her furniture from the living room into the spare bedroom before the workers came.

"I'm sorry. I fell asleep last night before I could get this done."

She said to a worker as she was lugging on her loveseat, "Could you please give me a hand?"

Her house was a mess. She felt very disorganized as she tried to get ready for work. "My briefcase, where is my briefcase?"

One of the workers lifted a tarp that was lying on the floor. "Is this it?" he asked as he held it up. "Yes, thank you. So will it be ready when I get home?" She smiled.

"Wishful thinking ma'am."

Mayla raced to the office in her little BMW. She was forty-five minutes late and needed to help Tom with the Riley case.

"He's going to be so pissed!" Mayla sped up the parking ramp to the garage where she quickly parked her car and ran into the office.

"Mr. Wheeler is looking for you Mayla." Snared the underpaid blond that sat at the front desk, "He's says its urgent that you get into his office as soon as you walk through the front door."

"Thank you Julia."

Mayla and Tom spent the entire morning working on the Riley case. As they broke for lunch Shelby ran to Mayla

"Mayla, you have to see what I received today!" She spoke as if she were singing. "Come with me!"

Shelby took Mayla by the hand and walked her to her office.

"Look!"

"At what?"

"On my desk! See! A rose!"

"Yes I see."

"It's from Robert! The card reads, hopefully I can deliver the other eleven in person, Robert."

"It's so romantic! He's so classy!"

"He sure is! And that is a beautiful rose Shelby! I don't think I've ever seen one so lovely! Are you going to call him?"

"Oh no, I may be promiscuous but I will not call him. If he sent this, he'll call."

"I have to go get a bite to eat. Would you like to join me?"

"Yes, let me grab my purse."

Shelby and Mayla headed down to a French restaurant on Las Olas Boulevard.

"How's the Riley case going?" Shelby asked as she devoured her salmon appetizer. "Tom seems to be stressing over this case today."

"Who could blame him. There's so many unanswered questions, things are not adding up."

"What do you mean?"

"Well you know I really can't talk about this Shelby."

"I know but," Shelby paused, "I need more water. Where's the damn waiter? I don't know why we always come here, the service is horrible."

"The food is great. That's why Shelby."

"So tell me what's going on? Oh come on Mayla, I'm the other partners legal secretary I can find out."

"Oh all right. Things just don't add up. We are not sure that Mr. Riley is fessing up to the whole truth. We have given him plenty of opportunity to do so but he swears he was the only one involved. We even told him he may receive a plea bargain for a lesser sentence if he confesses other persons are involved."

"Really? He won't budge?"

"He says he was the only one involved. Think about it Shelby, we are talking about insurance fraud resulting in over ten million dollars! This man lives in Plantation! Where is all of his money? He has no gambling problems, no drug addictions; yes he and his wife drive Mercedes but, to live in Plantion? Why not at least a house on the intercoastal with a big ass boat? That money went somewhere else. He was not the only one involved. If he can't tell his attorneys the truth and the FBI find other people are involved, we are going to be the laughing stock of the Florida Bar and we will never defend another person in this town again."

"So how did he steal over ten million dollars?"

"You are never going to believe this." Mayla replied as she held her glass up to the waiter, "He took out insurance policies for elderly people who were about to kick the bucket. He forged medical records; signatures and he used recently deceased people from different states as the beneficiary. He would get the newspaper from New York, New Jersey the East Coast and read the obituaries. Morbid don't you think?"

"How was he caught?"

"Someone from the bank knew the deceased person that he was opening an account for. They blew the whistle. He had their social security number, identification everything! What are the chances that someone would actually know this dead person? I just don't understand how one person can run this multi-million dollar scam. His wife knew nothing."

"How do you know?"

"She is under psychiatric care for attempting suicide."

"Come on Mayla, she knew."

"No, she was almost successful. She barely made it."

"Creepy! So, have they started on your house yet?"

"Today. I'll be going home to a mess. We need to go." Mayla said as she looked at her watch. "Tom will keep me all night if I stay a minute past the hour."

Mayla and Shelby made their way back to the office where the mailroom boys greeted them.

"Shelby, Ken and I would like to go to happy hour again this Friday. We scored big! We got a total of seven numbers between the two of us. And we both had dates for Saturday night. I didn't come home."

"Well I am very proud of the both of you Jimmy, but may I suggest that you keep those things covered up?"

"Always. You could invest your money in latex."

"Nice Jimmy. Very nice."

That evening Mayla arrived home after eight p.m. Tom had kept her in the office until seven o'clock that evening. She was greeted by a thunderstorm, which in turn caused a major pile up, on I-95.

"I wish these damn people would learn how to drive." She said to herself. "Every damn fricken day an accident. I live twenty minutes from the office and it takes me an hour and ten minutes to get home."

Mayla peered out her window as she started honking her horn at the car in front of her. It was obvious the woman found this accident to be most intriguing. Her neck was turned a full eighty degrees as she passed by.

"Move it! Move it! Read it in the gosh damn paper! Watch the news tonight!" Mayla began to lose her temper.

The woman sped up as she passed by the wreck. Mayla shook her head in disbelief. The worst drivers in the world must be sent to South Florida.

When Mayla reached home she was frightened to open her door to find what mess may greet her. Much to her surprise the construction workers left her condo in a livable condition. Mayla made her way to the freezer where she took out a frozen pizza and put it in the oven. She turned on her television and went to the shower.

The next morning came and when she arrived to her office Shelby was standing there grinning from ear to ear.

"What's happened?" Mayla asked.

"Lets get some coffee. Put your things down." Shelby grabbed Mayla's arm as they made their way to the kitchen.

"He called."

"Who?"

"Robert."

"And?"

"We are meeting tonight for drinks."

"Where?"

"That new Italian place on the ocean front."

"Giovanni's?"

"That's it! I'm so nervous! I may go home and change. This suit makes me look fat."

"You look great! Pass me the creamer please. What time are you meeting him?"

"Around six o'clock."

"You better call me when, damn it!" Mayla said as she spilt coffee on her hand, "Where are the paper towels? No paper towels? Jimmy and Ken are so concerned about seeing how many numbers they can get and getting laid they can't even keep the paper towels filled!" Mayla dried her hand on an old towel in the kitchen then turned to Shelby; "You better call me as soon as you leave the restaurant! And I want to see you before you go!"

"Yes mother!"

Shelby had a hard time concentrating on her work that day. It had been nearly two months since she has had a date aside from picking men up at happy hour.

"Shelby, I need you in my office." Michael called.

"Yes sir."

Shelby stood up and followed Michael into his office.

"What can I do for you?"

"I need to go to New York tonight. I need for you to arrange my flights. I will be meeting Max Simoni for dinner this evening."

"Why doesn't he ever come down here?"

"Shelby please." Michael said sternly. "Arrange the flights. I will also need you to drop the documents off for me at this address."

"When?"

"Now."

Shelby left Michael's office with the sealed white envelope in her hand. "Grump." She mumbled.

Max Simoni was the other partner that lived in New York and had another law office in the city. He is a very brilliant, wealthy man in his early fifties. He came to Michael and Tom when they were struggling to open their own practice a few years ago. Max wanted to start an office in South Florida as another business venture. So he called on the two most respected defense attorneys in Ft. Lauderdale. Max has had a total of seven visits in three years. The first visit was to help find the most prestigious office space in Ft. Lauderdale and to agree on a partnership. Max had agreed to foot the bill for the first year of business and then a percentage of the earnings there after.

Shelby picked up the handset to the phone and started dialing the travel agent that booked flights for them.

"Yes, is this Pamela?"

"It sure is. Whom is it that I am speaking with?"

"This is Shelby Peterson from Max, Devon and Wheeler."

"Oh yes, Shelby how are you?"

"I'm great thank you. Mr. Devon would like to book a flight to New York for this evening."

"My goodness, that man has been frequenting New York quite a bit lately!"

"Really? I wasn't aware."

Shelby made a face and continued as she picked up an ink pen.

"Yes, he was just there this weekend."

"Well I guess he needs to go again tonight."

"I have a flight leaving at four-thirteen."

"That should be just fine. Let me give you our corporate account number."

"Oh Shelby honey, we have that right here. Now would Mr. Devon like to pick these up at the airport?"

"That would be wonderful."

After Shelby finished making the arrangements for Michael's tickets she headed to the parking garage to deliver the envelope.

Michael was in his office preparing for his last minute meeting with Max. He was talking to himself.

"Don't forget the Platinum American Express. Don't forget my tie, don't forget to call my wife." He then punched the speaker button on his telephone and begun to dial.

"Honey? How are you?"

"Fine honey. How are you?"

"Listen, I'm sorry but I have to go to New York tonight. I need to have dinner with Max. We are having a problem with the contract with the building owners and we need to get it resolved. I'll be home in the morning."

"Honey I miss you. You were away over the weekend playing golf. I feel like I haven't seen you in."

"I know Marlene," Michael said as if he were begging, "just one more day. Kiss the girls for me. Tell them I love them. And honey when I get home we will go to your favorite restaurant and then this weekend you and I will go somewhere without the girls if your mom will watch them. I'm sorry honey. I don't mean to upset you."

"Promise me Michael."

"I promise."

"I love you."

"I love you too."

Michael hit the speaker button. There was silence in the room as he let out a sigh. He turned his chair to over look the view of the New River. The rain was coming down hard now. He sat for nearly a half an hour before realizing the afternoon storm had passed and the sun was peeking through the clouds.

"Key West." He spun his chair around and pressed the speakerphone where he called Tom's extension.

"Tom, its Michael. What's the name of the hotel in Key West that you always stay in? Uh huh? Do you have the number?"

Michael phoned the hotel.

"Hi I would like to make a reservation for this weekend. I need a room with a view and a bottle of your finest bottle of champagne on ice for our arrival."

And so it was. Michael and Marlene will spend the weekend in Key West.

Shelby arrived at the address on the envelope.

"What the heck, it's a mailbox place."

It was a storefront colored red and blue. Very patriotic. Shelby unhooked her seat belt and grabbed the envelope from the passenger seat then stepped out of her car. She glanced down one last time to check the address. Still unsure she walked in the store and asked the young man at the counter.

"I'm not sure if I." She began to speak but was interrupted.

"Yes you are in the right place."

"How did you know I was going to ask?"

"Listen when people have affairs they get P.O. boxes."

"I don't think my boss is having an affair."

"Miss, this is Ft. Lauderdale, everyone is having an affair."

The young skinny man behind the counter seemed to be very convincing.

"We'll see." Said Shelby as she smiled and turned away.

When she returned to the office she called Michael to confirm that it was a post office box. He agreed. There is no way Michael is having an affair! Never ever! Her first instinct was to pick up the phone and call Mayla.

"Mayla, I need to talk you."

"I can't right now."

"This is urgent. Please come to my office."

Mayla walk into Shelby's office where she sat down on the blue chair in front of Shelby.

"This better be good."

"It is. I think Michael is having an affair. At first I didn't believe it but."

"Oh my god." Mayla interrupted. "I thought so too."

"What do you mean?" Asked Shelby.

"He told me he was going to Orlando with his wife and the girls. I saw his wife in the hardware store on Saturday. She told me he went to play golf! I couldn't bring myself to say anything. I only asked how the girls were."

"Well it gets better. I just made reservations for him to go to New York this evening to meet with Max, when I called our travel agent she said he was a busy man! He was there this past weekend! Then," Shelby took a deep breath, "he had me deliver a white envelope to a post office box at that postal store on US1. The guy behind the counter says that people use those places for affairs! Basically a way of communicating I guess."

"I really hope this is not happening. I like Michael so much."

"Me too." Shelby replied, "But we need to just play it cool and stay out of his business."

"You're right!"

Mayla left Shelby's office with an empty sad feeling in her stomach. She always looked up to Michael and envied his life. He is a prominent attorney who was happily married with two beautiful girls. It just didn't seem right.

Later that afternoon Shelby was in her office beginning to feel the butterflies come about in her stomach.

"Oh my. A date." She said to herself. "How will I act? This man seems to be so intellectual, so smart. I made it through college by the skin of my teeth!" Shelby glanced at her watch and said, "I can't even be on time!" She picked up her phone and dialed extension twelve.

"Mayla?"

"Wish me luck. I'm so nervous. I don't know why! I feel as if I'm going to get diarrhea."

"You are so gross Shelby. Just pinch your cheeks and smile."

"I'm leaving."

"Good luck."

Shelby parked behind the restaurant and dug through her purse for change. There was a knock on her window that startled her so badly she dropped the coins. It was Robert smiling through the window.

"Hi!" Shelby smiled back.

"Hello Miss Peterson." Replied Robert as he opened her door, "I saw this beautiful woman drive around the corner, she caught my eye so I sought after her. What happiness it brought me when I saw it was you."

Robert took Shelby's hand and helped her out of the car.

Shelby smiled and simply said, "thank you."

"You look wonderful. How was your day?"

"It was great. How was yours?"

"Very busy and productive! I know I startled you and made you drop your change so allow me to fill this meter for you."

Robert dug into his pocket and pulled out a fist full of change.

"While I was waiting for you I noticed this restaurant seems to be quite busy. I know of another where the food is wonderful and the wine is plentiful. We can leave your car here. I'll drive."

The restaurant was only a few blocks west. It was a small French bistro with large windows and a red with white striped awnings above them. On the inside a tiny woman with a heavy French accent greeted them.

"Two for dinner?"

"Yes please." Robert replied as he held his arm out to lead Shelby, "Mademoiselle after you."

They sat at a small round table with a red checked tablecloth. The waiter brought fresh sourdough rolls and creamy butter. "May I tell you about our specials?" He asked as he handed the wine list to Robert.

"Please."

The waiter was also French. As he rattled off the specials Robert kept his eyes focused on Shelby. He was actually cooing. It was almost as if the waiter was non existent. Shelby's heart was pattering as she tried to remain cool. This was not the usual man she would attract. They were generally the types that were looking for a quick lay. Robert seemed different. A gentleman. Throughout dinner they talked about where they were from, they're family backgrounds and traveling.

"Have you ever been to Europe?" Robert asked.

"A few times."

"Really? Where have you been?"

Shelby's eyes lit up when she recalled her memories of her trips. "I've only been to Paris, Rome, Frankfurt and London. Twice."

"I love to travel." Replied Robert; "Maybe I could persuade you to come with me sometime. Is your passport current?"

"Yes of course." *Is my passport current?* She though to herself. *Wouldn't that be exciting, travel around the world with this handsome man?*

After dinner Robert drove Shelby back to her car. He walked around to the passenger side and opened her door.

"Thank you for a wonderful evening Miss Peterson."

"I had a great time. Dinner was delicious, thank you."

Robert walked Shelby to her car where she had a parking ticket waiting for her.

"Oh darn it." Shelby said.

"I got it." Robert demanded as he grabbed the ticket from her, "I'll have my secretary send it in and use it as a write off."

"That's convenient."

Robert leaned towards Shelby as he grabbed her chin and planted a kiss on her cheek. "Be careful going home."

He stood and watched Shelby drive off before he settled into his shiny black Ferrari Spider.

CHAPTER THREE

"How was your pasta Michael? I told you they have the best clam sauce in New York."

"It was very good."

"Did you bring the papers I asked you for Michael?" inquired Max.

"Yes." He replied as he looked across the table at the man he despised. "Of course I did. They are in my briefcase. And I am also expecting an envelope."

"Very well." Max reached into his inner pocket of suit where he pulled out a white envelope and placed it on the table, "This should be accurate. Count it."

"I don't believe that is necessary." Michael placed the envelope on the table next to him.

"Good."

Max reached for a cigar that was sitting on the white linen tablecloth. He snipped the end and carefully rolled it around on his tongue. "Do I have anything to worry about?"

"Such as?"

"Michael, do I have anything to be concerned about?"

"No Max. You have nothing to be concerned about. However, the office staff would like to see more of you."

"I will be down. I need to work on my tan."

The smell of the cigar began to bother Michael. He pushed his chair away from the table and excused himself to make a phone call.

"Honey? Can you hear me?" Michael walked out on the brutally hot streets of New York to get some fresh air and telephone his wife. "I just called to say I miss you. Kiss the girls and I will see you tomorrow."

Michael took one last deep breath of fresh air as he retrieved the antenna to his cell phone and put it in his front pocket of his navy blue slacks. "There is no way out."

As he seated himself the waiter was quick to put his napkin on his lap.

"Cappuccino? Espresso?"

"Just the check please."

"Have an espresso Michael we're not through yet."

"I don't need an espresso."

"Very well. The check then please." Max smiled at the waiter and then turned his head to Michael. "I hope Philipo has nothing to worry about."

"Philipo has nothing to worry about Max." Michael said as he put his napkin on the table and stood up. "I'm sure I will be talking to you."

Michael walked outside where he hailed himself a yellow taxicab. Max stayed behind to finish his espresso.

Max had a way of casually upsetting people. And when he was angry, he had a very thoughtful was of being so. Those who worked for him were frightened of him. And due to his money and candidness all the women adored him.

CHAPTER FOUR

The Following morning in Ft. Lauderdale was brutal. It was so muggy you could see the moisture in the air and practically cut it with a knife. Not a good day for anyone with hair.

"Mayla!" Shelby waved across the parking garage. "I think I'm in love!"

"Oh brother, here we go." Mayla mumbled to herself. "Tell me what happened."

Shelby walked closer toting her handbag, briefcase and coffee. "It was wonderful! We had dinner and wine, we talked forever. He seems too good to be true."

"Maybe he is."

"I don't think so. I just don't understand what a guy like that wants with a girl like me. He's so well groomed in life. He's very smart, polite, I really don't know how to say this but, I feel uneducated around him."

"Shelby, please don't underestimate yourself."

"Press the elevator button Mayla my hands are full. I don't think I'm underestimating myself."

"Is there a second date?"

"If I have anything to do with it there will be."

"Just don't sleep with him Shelby. Not if you like him. Wait at least a few more dates."

"God Mayla you make me sound like a slut."

"You're not a slut, but you are a bit easy. The last guy, what was his name? Jeff or George? You did him the first night and he never called again. You were certain he was different, magical. I remember that one!"

"Okay Mayla. No sex. At least not for a few dates."

Shelby and Mayla walked into the office where they were greeted with somber faces.

"What has happened?" asked Mayla.

No one answered. They all continued looking at Mayla with a dead stare.

"Will someone please tell me what happened?" Mayla put her hand on her hip, "Where's Tom? Why is no one answering me?"

Mayla's heart began to skip beats. She walked past the reception area and headed towards Tom's office. Upon arrival she saw Tom standing there with a man from Broward County Sheriff's office.

"Tom?"

"Someone broke into the office Mayla."

"What? Who?"

"We don't know. They didn't get too much. Just a couple computers and a VCR in the conference room." Tom sighed and looked at the Sheriff, "they destroyed your office and mine."

"What?"

Mayla turned her back to head towards her office.

"Mayla wait!"

Mayla continued walking. Upon her arrival she found pictures of her family scattered on the floor. Her desk drawers were wide open. Then there was the icebreaker, the idiot that did this wrote "free me" on a picture of Vermin her bird, then taped it on the window.

"Sick." She said as she stood in the middle of her office.

"Ma'am." Asked the officer. "We'll need that picture for evidence."

"Do we have any idea at all as to who did this? Anything? Why my office Tom? Why your office Tom?"

"I don't know."

"Well," said the officer, "Your two offices were the only ones that were locked."

"What does that have to do with anything?" Asked Mayla.

"The thief must have found this to be a challenge to get into your office. He wasn't happy that you two locked your doors, so when he got in he thought he would leave you a little surprise. That's our guess anyway."

"He was upset we locked our offices? That sounds a little ridiculous."

"Maybe so. There will be some finger printing so try not to touch anything. I would suggest you send your employees out for coffee and bagels while we do our job. We don't want anyone disrupting anything. After we are done here I want Mayla and Tom to check for any personal items you might be missing. Remember this is also a law firm that defends the scum of South Florida, and well, your not gong to win any awards for humanity. You help set a lot of criminals free on technicalities. I know we don't like it. So try to think of anyone that may be upset with the firm."

"That could be anyone." Tom shook his head.

"We've defended so many people. It could be someone related to the Gonzelez family. Their son is doing eighteen years on drug related charges. That boy got himself in so much trouble, we just couldn't help them anymore." Mayla mumbled to herself

"Or maybe it was a simple robbery Mayla."

BSO's crime scene unit stayed most of the day dusting for fingerprints, looking for anything that may have been left behind in the parking garage and also checking security cameras. The video tapes showed there was no one in the garage after Mr. Ballini from the third floor left around nine p.m. So the thief must have parked in front of the building. But the videotape had shown no one entering or leaving the front door after seven p.m.

Michael called Tom on his cell phone before he left from New York. "I'll pick you up from the airport. Hopefully I will have some type of news for you."

Michael had several drinks on the airplane. The woman seated next to him had a baby on her lap and when he leaned over to play with the baby she asked to be moved.

"My world is falling apart." He said to himself. "My wife is unhappy, my partner is about to cause problems and now this."

It was just three years ago that he helped form his law firm. In such a short time they found themselves defending some of the most high profile cases in the State of Florida. Several times the firm had found themselves being interviewed by the local television stations and once Tom was interviewed on the Today Show in New York for defending the largest real-estate scam in Florida history.

"My god this place is a mess." Michael said as he passed through the reception door. "Did they have to rip the whole fucking office apart? And let me guess? No suspects. No one to pin the blame on! Whoever it was picked the wrong office to rob."

Michael stomped off to his office.

Tom stood in disbelief as he watched Michael from the distance. Michael had left his office door open and made such a display when he pushed everything off his cherry wood desk. He then opened a drawer where he pulled out his favorite cognac used for celebrations and drank it straight from the bottle. Michael looked up and saw Tom standing there. Without taking his eyes off Tom he walked towards the door and slammed it.

"That man needs a vacation." Tom said shaking his head.

Two days had passed and the investigation was going slow. The only thing that BSO had discovered is that there were no identifiable fingerprints. The office had almost returned to normal except they still needed to replace the VCR in the conference room.

"Michael," Tom said into his telephone. "I have a presentation this afternoon and need to replace the VCR. I'm going to pick one up, would you like to ride with me?"

"Yes I would. Maybe we can have lunch. I would like to discuss some issues with you."

"Okay meet me in my office at eleven."

Tom's intuition was the same as Mayla's and Shelby's. Maybe he was going to come clean with his affair that he had been having. It was obviously disturbing him enough to put on such a display at the office. Michael's mild mannerisms have been put to a test. Tom was certain he was going to have an opportunity to find out who she was and how he got involved with her. How did she look? Was she a beautiful woman? How did they meet? Maybe Marlene found out and is planning to leave him.

"Tom?" Mayla asked as she poked her head around the corner, "I am telling you that something is not right with Mr. Riley. I just received this from the Judd Haverin's office and it's more evidence against Mr. Riley. This one shows him collecting a life insurance policy under the alias of Warren Fitz, a dead man from Century Village. The total dollar amount he collected? Look." Mayla pointed to the paper. "Five-hundred-thousand. Where in hell is the money?"

"I don't know, but I have feeling we are going to lose our asses. I hope he can afford us."

"According to his personal bank accounts he can't."

"He must have money hidden somewhere else and he is not telling us about it."

"Well I hope this doesn't unfold while we are at trial. We won't look good!" Mayla said as she picked up the folder and turned to the door.

"Hey Mayla?"

"Yes?" She turned to look at Tom.

"Anyone going to happy hour?"

"I think so. You're invited."

She smiled as she walked out his door and met Michael.

"Hi Michael. How are you? Are you getting ready to go away this weekend?"

"I certainly am! Only a few more hours." He seemed excited.

"I guess no happy hour for you today."

"Not today Mayla."

Michael walked into Tom's office and sat on the chair in front of his desk.

"What are you working on?"

"I'll give you one guess." Tom replied.

"Ok, the Riley case."

"Good guess. This guy is not coming clean with us. He is going to do some hard time. Every time I turn around there's new evidence against him. How can we possibly represent him when he is not being straight with us? According to his personal financial statements he has about one hundred and fifty thousand dollars in the bank a few stocks that are not doing that well, and a few savings bonds. Look at this. Have you ever seen anything like it?"

Tom turned the Riley file toward Michael.

"You see? Yes he has some assets. A few pieces of art here and there. His house does not have a mortgage, but it's a three hundred thousand-dollar home. Can you believe the Mercedes that he and his wife each have are on a lease? I don't get it. He stole ten million dollars! If he doesn't come clean with us we can't represent him! I'm ready to tell him to."

"Before you go on, I need to discuss something with you Tom."

He is going to come clean about his affair. Good. Now he will be a bit more tolerable.

"Yes?" Asked Tom

"It has to do with the Riley case. It's why I haven't exactly been myself lately."

"What is it Michael?" Tom was becoming antsy. He knew he was withholding information on the case.

Michael stood up and walked over to the window to admire the view and avoid eye contact with Tom.

"Michael? I wish someone would come clean with me on this case because I'm about to drop the damn thing! I will not go to trial without a case! This guy is a damn idiot! He wants me to play private investigator and he is the one I have to investigate because he won't tell me a fucking thing! Now you come in here and tell me you need to talk to me about this case! What and the hell do you know?" Tom's voice was growing louder and he was becoming more impatient. "Tell me Michael."

"Paul Riley is a friend of Max's."

"What? What are you talking about?" Tom stood up and walked towards Michael, "you better clue me in."

"It's why I have had to go to New York to meet with Max." Michael sighed, "he's very serious about us representing this guy."

"Why am I just finding this out?"

"Tom I knew about this only two weeks ago. You know the meetings we always have with Max on Mondays; well do you remember we told him about the Riley case? We told him it was not going well and we were thinking about dropping him because he was not helping us out?"

"Yes of course. But why did he ask you and not me?"

"Max thinks you have some type of animosity towards him. He didn't want to tell me either. But when we told him we were about to drop this case. He wanted me in New York immediately! I had to tell Marlene I was going to play golf! She gets upset with me when I work so late and on the weekends. In your confidence Tom, she does not care for Max. She thinks you are great but she also thinks Max is more of a dictator than a partner. I can't always tell her what I am doing and to be honest Tom it's putting a lot of pressure on me."

I'm just trying to keep this firm strong and happy. I feel like a damn yo-yo between you, my wife and Max.

Tom felt a sense of guilt rush over him as Michael sat down on the mole hair sofa that sat below a painting from the Las Olas art festival.

"Does he know the stress it is putting on this firm?"

"I'm sure he does, Paul Riley and Max grew up together. Max's father apparently worked for Paul's father as a chef in an Italian restaurant. Paul's father became very close to Max's. It was Paul's father that put

Max through law school. Max's father was very poor. He had to support a family with six children. He feels he has a very large debt to pay."

"I understand now. I just wish it was brought out in the open sooner."

"Max is a very private person Tom. You know that. I told him I couldn't hold it in any longer. He understands that Paul Riley is not being very helpful. He just wants us to represent him the best we can. And if he won't come clean, well then how are we to help?"

"That's fair. But Michael, I won't go crazy on this anymore."

Tom began to laugh as he placed his hand on Michael's shoulder, "I thought you were having an affair."

"Are you kidding?"

"No I'm not! Mayla saw your wife at the hardware store last Saturday."

"She did?" Michael's face grew with concern.

"Don't worry." Tom smiled, "she did not speak a word. I'll have a talk with her about this later. I need to tell her of this obstacle we have incurred."

"I guess that will be fine. But tell her not to discuss this one with other employees."

"Not a problem. I'm hungry. Where would you like to eat?"

Tom and Michael both remained silent as they walked to the restaurant.

CHAPTER FIVE

Shelby was reading her e-mail when Mayla interrupted her. "Want to go to lunch?"

"Sure let me finish this really quick."

"What are you reading?" Mayla asked as she walked closer. "Gossip?"

"As a matter of fact it seems that Kenny our little misbehaved mailroom boy, maybe in a bit of trouble."

"How's that?"

"We maybe having a baby shower for him."

"What!"

"Yep. Seems he scored big with a happy hour girl."

"Yikes. Poor guy. And he said he wore protection."

"Not always fool proof Mayla."

"True."

Shelby's face began to draw a smile. "I have a date this evening."

"Robert called?"

"Yes he sure did." Shelby responded as she grabbed her purse.

"Where are you going?"

"To dinner. Some French place in Boca."

"Sounds very romantic!"

"Is he picking you up?"

"You bet. I'll be twirling around in my living room awaiting his arrival." She sang, "seven. He'll pick me up at seven. What about you girl? What are you doing tonight?"

"Well I thought about going to happy hour but no one else is going. You have a date. Michael is going to Key West with his wife, or so he says and I'm sure Kenny and Jimmy are going to keep their little pee pee's in their pockets for a while."

"Ask Tom."

"Tom will want a date." Mayla replied firmly.

"Jeez Mayla, not everyone wants in your pants."

"I guess there is no harm in a movie."

"Any suggestions on where we should go for lunch? I'll be having French tonight so how about that Italian place down the street?"

"Sounds good."

When Shelby and Mayla arrived at the restaurant Michael and Tom greeted them.

"Hello ladies." Tom said with a smirk.

"You know Tom," Mayla said as she clenched her jaw, "You are so nice, normal and professional at work but get on the elevator and as it descends from floor to floor, the more of a pig you become. I was going to ask you to the movies but I am thinking that for my safety I best not." She shook her head at him.

The host approached the foursome. "Four for lunch?"

"Ladies?" Michael asked, "Care to join us?"

"Only if Tom behaves." Mayla responded.

"Please." Cried Tom, "I'll be good Mayla. I promise!"

"This is not at date." She replied as she turned to look at him. "I mean it. It's just a movie."

"I know." Tom hung his head and smiled.

"I hope they bring that bread." Mayla said as she pulled her chair to sit down.

"So what does everyone have planned for the weekend?" Asked Michael.

"Mayla and I are going to the movies tonight and that's all I care about!"

"Tom!" Mayla scolded, "Settle down."

"Settling."

"I have a date." Shelby said proudly, "With Robert in Boca at some fancy French restaurant."

"Let's go spy Mayla. Instead of going to the movies."

"No."

"OK." Tom backed down.

"Is it raining again?" asked Shelby as she peered out the window. "I've had enough. My hair is going to be frizzy for my date tonight."

"Wear it up Shelby." Said Michael; "It's a little more mysterious when a woman pins her hair up."

"I'll take your advice Michael."

"So what can you tell us about this guy? Aside from the fact that he drives a Ferrari?" Michael stuffed a piece of bread in his mouth.

"One day you'll get to meet him."

After lunch Mayla and Shelby returned to the office and Tom and Michael went to the electronics store to purchase a VCR. Things would slowly return to normal; however, there were still no leads on the robbery.

3

CHAPTER SIX

Robert arrived in his black Ferrari. The doorbell rang and Shelby walked down the steps of her townhouse to answer the door. Her heart was racing and she felt her face begin to flush as she peered through the peephole. She took a deep breath and opened the door.

"Hello." She flashed a smile.

"Good evening." Robert replied with a smile, "How was your day?"

"It was good. Would you like to come in for a cocktail before dinner?"

"That would be nice."

"What would you like?"

"What do you have?"

"How about if I surprise you." *Good idea* Shelby thought to herself, *he would probably ask for something I don't have. That would be embarrassing.*

"Great idea. You have a nice home Shelby."

"Thank you." She yelled from the kitchen, "I decorated it myself."

Robert remained standing by the front door and the steps leading upstairs.

"Please, come in and sit down." Shelby said as she brought the cock-tails from the kitchen, "I hope vodka cranberry is alright."

"That is just perfect."

"Did you come straight from your office?" Shelby asked as she sat down and placed her drink on her cocktail table.

"I had a fairly busy day today. The market was so unstable and for a broker to work past six on a Friday is very unlikely. So the answer to your question is yes."

"So you know what it's like for the rest of the world."

Shelby began to tease him as she handed him his cocktail.

He sipped his drink and placed in on the glass coffee table in front of him.

"How is it?" She asked.

"Great."

Robert couldn't take his eyes off her. He found himself losing his composure. This woman excited him. He was gazing at her hair that had been swept up by a single pin. He continued examining the short light blue dress that complimented her eyes.

"You look very nice."

"You're always so full of wonderful things to say Robert. If you're not careful, I'm going to become very conceded." Shelby didn't know how to respond to his compliments.

"I sincerely doubt that will ever happen Miss Peterson."

"Don't."

There was a silence. Robert continued investigating her long silky legs. He started to fantasize about how he would make love to her for the first time. He wishes it could be tonight. "*I must take this slowly.*" He thought to himself.

"How is you drink?"

There was no answer.

"Robert, how is your drink?"

Robert was embarrassed to find that Shelby caught him day dreaming about her.

"It's the best vodka cranberry I have ever had. Are you ready for dinner?"

"I sure am."

The glasses were left behind on the table. Shelby searched for her purse then she locked the door behind them as they left for the restaurant.

"Hi Mayla. Come here. Pretend you love me." Tom said as he greeted Mayla in front of the movie theater in Pompano Beach.

"I'm warning you Tom! Don't get fresh with me, I have laundry that needs to be done!"

"I'll behave. But let me buy the movie."

"Deal."

"So what would you like to see Mayla? Let me guess, the new chick movie starring Grace Donovan."

"No, actually I would like to see that testosterone movie with the army tanks."

"Darn. I was hoping to see the chick movie. I thought it may soften your heart."

"My heart is soft."

"Then you buy the popcorn."

"Give me a raise." She was firm.

After Tom purchased the tickets to the movie they stood in the concession stand line to get the popcorn.

"I talked to Michael today."

"What about?"

"I told him that the whole office thought he was having an affair. I told him that you were very upset."

"You did not!" She smacked him on the shoulder.

"At any rate, he's not having an affair. Apparently he has been flying to New York to deal with Max."

"And he has to lie about it?" She questioned.

"I guess Marlene's not a big fan of Max's either."

"How's that?"

"This really needs to remain confidential."

"I can keep quiet. Now talk to me."

"Paul Riley is a good friend to Max and his family. Max owes his family a favor. It was Paul's father who put Max through law school. He knows we are going to lose the case with all the evidence that he has built up against him, he just wants us to try to get a lesser sentence."

"Is that why Michael has been so unbearable?"

"Yes. After all, Max funded this law firm. Without him, the law firm would not exist."

"It's making sense now. But why isn't anyone else to know about this?"

"Max likes to keep his private life private."

"I understand." Mayla moved up to the concession stand, "Hi large popcorn no butter and two medium cokes."

Mayla turned to Tom as she grabs the popcorn and drinks.

"Let me help you." He said.

"Thanks. So Michael should be back to normal?"

"I hope so. By the way, he was in New York with Max when he was supposed to be in Orlando. Marlene thinks he works too hard. So he told her he was going on a golf weekend with some friends."

"Poor Michael."

"I would say so."

"Shelby." Robert asked as he looked at her from across the table and held her hand, "I must confess to you. When we were at your house having cocktails, I was fantasizing about the way I would make love to you for the first time. I know you must be a very passionate women. Am I being a little too forward for only our second date?"

Shelby nearly choked on her wine.

"I'm not sure how to respond to something like that Robert. I've never had anyone be so honest about, well, that before." She had a hard time saying it, making love. She thought it was a gross way of covering up the truth about sex. *It's sex Robert. Just sex. We can talk about sex, sex, sex. Not love. Not yet anyway.*

"I can't help myself."

Shelby's heart began to race as she found herself wanting to crawl under the table to satisfy him.

"I can make this man very happy right now. I could float into my own world, let myself go. Make him feel like he has never been with a woman before until me. I want to devour this man. I will devour this man. In my time." She thought to herself.

"Shelby," Robert looked in her eyes and reached for her other hand, "I have to go away next week on Thursday, would it be possible for you to join me?"

"Of course I will join you. I want to have you from dusk to dawn. Ravage you. I will make you feel like Adam did when he first touched Eve. How joyous that must have been. For both of them." Shelby's inner thoughts were getting carried away with her. Then she spoke.

"Where would we be going and for how long?"

"I need to go to London for a week. Can you join me? If you're not comfortable I will get you your own room."

"Not comfortable? I wouldn't go unless I knew we would consummate this relationship. If it means traveling to Europe so be it. I hope the mile high club is excepting applications right now." Stop talking to yourself Shelby, he may hear you.

The wine was beginning to take over. She felt her body grow warm. *"Take control Shelby. Stop fantasizing! You may lose yourself at the table. Shelby you're becoming more and more excited. What I would give to have him reach under this table and pleasure me. Please take me somewhere Robert, we don't need an airplane or car to get there. I only need you. Any part of you. Your tongue, mouth."*

"Robert I would love to go but I'm not sure I can get away."

"Please ask. I would love to spend some time with you."

"I will talk with my boss."

"I will beg my boss. I will tell him how I Shelby Peterson is going on a romantic getaway filled with exploring the inner caves of the human body that god has so graciously given us."

"Very well then, I would like to make a toast. To the most beautiful woman I have ever met."

Shelby wanted him so badly she couldn't control herself. She felt herself getting more and more excited. All he had to do was touch her under her panties just once and she would climax to an orgasm that would put any woman that ever had one to shame. She excused herself and went to the restroom where she stopped the excitement. She had to wait to sleep with him.

After dinner Robert walked Shelby to her front door and placed his hands on her face. "May I kiss you goodnight?"

"I would be disappointed if you didn't."

Robert then pressed his lips against hers. It was a very slow subtle kiss. He did not share his tongue. Not yet.

"Would you like to come in?"

"Not tonight. I have an early tee-time tomorrow."

Robert turned to walk to his car.

After the movie Tom and Mayla returned to the diner they were at on Saturday night.

"I wonder how Shelby's date is going?" Tom asked as he dipped a French fry in ketchup. "Think she's getting any?"

"I'm sure we will find out tomorrow morning. At least I will."

"Come on Mayla, don't you want me?"

"Tom, you disgust me, okay? I like to work for you, but you are repulsive. I could never find myself in bed with a man of your likes. My mother would be so unhappy if I ever brought home someone like you."

"Oh, ouch!" Tom said as he grabbed his chest. "You are hurting me so badly Mayla. Please stop."

Mayla fished out an ice cube from her water and threw it at him. "Cool off pal!"

"Mayla you are a lot of fun to tease!"

"Okay Tom, leave me alone."

Michael and Marlene had flown down to the Keys for the adventurous get away. The hotel had greeted them with the champagne that Michael had requested. After they had settled in they ventured around the island to Mallory Square where they would watch the vibrant sunset and death-defying fire-eaters. Then they would wonder into the small shops where Marlene would try on outfits for Michael. She would come out of the dressing room each time smiling. She walked towards him and then spun like a ballerina showing off the white sundress he picked for her.

Marlene stopped spinning when she noticed Michael's intent stare.

"Honey?" she asked.

"You're beautiful Marlene. I could never replace you. Nor would I want to. I'm so happy you are mine. I think I am falling in love all over again. Thank you for being so patient with me. Thank you for always loving me."

Marlene's eyes began to water. The young unmarried clerk stood by in envy.

"I love you too."

The rest of the evening was spent in the hotel room.

CHAPTER SEVEN

"Hello?" Answered Shelby.

"Hello Shelby." It was Robert. "Do you have anytime to spare tomorrow? I would like to see you. Maybe for lunch."

"Sure. What time?"

"Say around eleven? I'll pick you up."

"I have a better idea," Shelby said with excitement, "I'll make you lunch. It will be a surprise."

"I'd like that. Can I bring anything?"

"No just you. How was your golf game today?"

"It would have been better if it weren't for the rain. The lightning was so bad we had to stop on the fourteenth hole. It's a shame my game was going well."

"Sorry to hear that. I'll talk to mother nature for you."

"Do you have a special relationship with her?"

"I do. I have special relationships with all the gods."

"I'm glad I know you. I may ask for your help in the future."

"How's that?"

"I will let you know when and if I need help."

"Okay Robert."

"Then I will see you tomorrow?"

"Eleven o'clock."

"Good bye Shelby."

"Good bye Robert."

After hanging up the phone with Robert, Shelby immediately dialed Mayla's number.

"Hey Mayla it's Shelby, pick up the phone I know you're there! I need to talk to you. It's about Robert."

"Hey Shelby. Tell me. Tell me. Tell me."

"Well first of all last night was incredible! He thinks I'm beautiful! I know I must sound crazy but I've never met anyone so charming before!"

"You better be careful Shelby, you just met that guy. Don't let your heart get involved so quickly. It just might get broken."

"Oh Mayla, you don't understand! He asked me to go away with him! He is leaving for London on Thursday for business and he wants me to join him!"

"Wow! Okay, if that were me, I would be out of here in a heartbeat. Do you think Michael will let you go?"

"I don't see why he wouldn't. He might frown if you or Tom went somewhere with the big Riley case but we don't have anything major going on now that requires my constant assistance. I think he would be happy to see me go."

"Is he paying for your ticket?"

"I'm sure he is. He invited me. Oh and get this, he said I could have my own room if I wasn't comfortable. What a gentleman!"

"Did you call your Mom yet?"

"Not yet. But I will as soon as I hang up the phone."

"You definitely need to go on this trip Shelby. You will have a great time."

"I'm planning on it." She said excitedly.

"Make sure you give me the name and number of the hotel you will be staying at."

"I will. What are you doing tonight?"

"I don't have any plans. How about you?"

"Nothing. Want to rent a movie or go to the mall?"

"Sure."

"What did you do last night?"

"I went to the movie with Tom."

"He has a date tonight with some girl he met in the grocery store."

"Really? He never told me that!"

"I think he has a secret crush on you Mayla. I just bet that's why he didn't want to tell you."

"He's a pig."

"I think it's a cover up. I bet he's a real softy. You should know. How long have you worked for him?"

"Couple of years."

"Mayla, that boy has it bad for you."

"Alright Shelby, that's enough. What time will you be over?"

"I'll come now."

Mayla and Shelby spent the rest of the day shopping for Shelby's London trip.

CHAPTER EIGHT

Monday morning came quickly. It was still raining and muggy. Traffic on I-95 was fierce as it was backed up for miles leading into the downtown area. There had been another accident where apparently a semi-truck had turned over on a car leaving some poor man dead. He probably had a family.

"When will this rain ever stop? I can't stand it anymore." Mayla mumbled as she picked up her cell phone and called into the office.

"Julia it's Mayla. Has Tom arrived?"

"Not yet. There's been an accident on I-95."

"Very good. I'll try him on his cell. Thank you."

Mayla pressed the "END" key on her cell phone and scanned for Tom's number that was programmed in her phone.

"Tom? How far are you from the office?"

"Far." He replied with frustration. "Mr. Riley will be waiting for us. I hope Julia is kind enough to offer him coffee."

"I'm sure she will Tom. I'm at dead stop. So I'll see you when I get in. Oh and before I hang up Tom, how was your date?"

This was the first time Tom was embarrassed by Mayla. He felt as if he were caught doing something wrong.

"It was fine."

"Fine? Is that all you can tell me? Fine? Tom, I thought you had all this stamina! I was waiting for you to tell me you romanced her until the cows came home. That she immediately fell in love with you. That she called her mother from your cell phone and told her what a wonderful time she was having and to get her an updated list of the relatives addresses so she could send them an invitation." Teasing him made her ride into work a bit more pleasurable even though she felt a tinge of jealousy.

"Come on Mayla, you know I am a true gentleman. I would never kiss and tell."

"Oh yes you are Tom. Yes you are."

"See you in the office."

"Wait! So did you?"

"Did I what?"

"Get some sugar."

"I've never heard you speak like that before."

"Like what?" She drew a smile as she gripped the steering wheel.

"Did I get any? Shame on you."

"Shame on me? You always talk like that. Well?"

"I'll never tell. Why, are you the jealous type?"

"Jealous? Of what?" Mayla cringed.

"Yep, you are."

"Fine, I'll see you when I get in."

As the rain continued to fall, Mayla and Tom would be stuck in traffic for nearly another hour before they arrived at the firm.

"Michael wants to see you." Julia rose her head long enough to see who walked through the glass door. "He said it was urgent."

"Thanks."

Shelby grabbed her mail that was sitting on Julia's desk as she headed to Michael's office.

"Michael? You want to see me?"

'Yes, I need you to deliver this envelope to this address for me."

"It appears it needs to go to the same place as the last one."

"It is."

"It will be my pleasure Michael!"

"It will?"

"Yes. I need to talk to you." Shelby said as she sat down on the chair sitting in front of Michael's desk, "I was hoping, or wondering rather. I have been invited to go to London on Thursday, I know it's short notice but it's a once in a lifetime chance and."

Michael interrupted. "Who will you be going with?"

"Robert."

"Robert seems to be quite smitten with you Shelby. Are you sure about this?"

"Absolutely!"

"I don't see why you can't go but how long will you be gone?"

"Only a week." Shelby's face grew with excitement, as she sensed Michael was going to let her go. "Please?"

"Yes Shelby you may go." Michael smiled as he watched her pop out of the chair.

"I'll deliver this right away."

"Thank you."

Without stopping in the lunchroom for a cup of coffee Shelby went back out into the rain with her large white envelope. She sat in her car she dialed Robert's private number in his office so she did not have to go through the switchboard to locate him.

"Hello?" answered a sweet low voice that made her knees quiver.

"Robert? Good morning it's Shelby." She said cheerfully.

"Well good morning. How are you today?"

"I am wonderful." She was starring ahead at the cement walls as if it was Robert, "I have great news, Michael is allowing me to join you in London! He didn't even flinch when I asked to go! I can't wait to start packing."

"That is just wonderful. You have just made my day. I will arrange for your tickets and have them sent to your office. I hope you don't mind, but since I live in Miami and we'll be flying out of that airport, would it be alright to meet you there?"

"Of course that will be fine."

"I will have a car pick you up."

"That would be nice. Do you know the time of the flight?"

"I believe the flight leaves around eight p.m."

"I will be impatiently waiting."

"So will I Miss Peterson. Say, before you hang up Shelby, I know it's short notice but do you have any plans for this evening? I'd like to take you to dinner. I know a great Italian pizza place up in Delray. It's far but I promise you a great pizza and the wine's not so bad."

"Sure. Why not? Around seven-thirty?"

"I was hoping six. I'm excited to see you."

"I will see you at six p.m. Mr. Edwards."

"Very well then. Have a great day. I'm looking forward to seeing you."

Shelby slowly depressed the END key with her index finger and held the palm of her other hand to her heart. She felt her stomach tremble with excitement as her infatuation was turning to something more exciting and invigorating. For a moment she thought of what it was that Robert had that could capture her attention, could it be his money? *I hope not.* Could it be his mannerism? His age? His physic? He had so much confidence. Most men Shelby had ever been with didn't have much character at all. They were simply interested in one thing. A quick lay or two and never to be seen again. What did Robert have?

Just as Shelby was about to back out of her parking spot she saw Mayla pull up in her car.

Waving her left arm out her window Shelby began a very unlady like yell.

"Mayla! Hey!"

As Mayla grew close she began to speak.

"What's up Shelby? I don't have much time, I have a meeting with Tom and Mr. Riley this morning."

Shelby sensed her need to rush.

"I have the okay by Michael to go to London!"

"That's great! Let's have lunch today and we can talk about it then. Where are you going?"

"I have to drop this envelope for Michael at the postal store on Federal Highway."

"What's it for?"

"Beats me. I thought this is how he communicated his affair that he's not having."

"Well be careful, there's a big storm cloud coming."

"Of course there is."

The summer months in South Florida were very unpredictable with the weather. The sky could be clear one minute and the next you would be fighting with Mother Nature. No one ever left home without an umbrella.

As Shelby disembarked from the parking garage she was greeted by the storm that Mayla told her about. It was very dark and windy. The pounding rain had just begun.

"Great."

Shelby fought the downpour with her wipers slamming from side to side on her windshield as she made her way through the flooded streets to the postal office. Taillights reflected on her windshield from the cars in front of her.

As she struggle to open her umbrella and get out the car the white envelope managed to swindle it's way out of her hands and into a big puddle of rain.

"Shit." Shelby said as she picked up the envelope and shook it off. "Shit. Michael's gonna kill me. He's such a damn perfectionist."

When she opened the front door of the postal store the same young man as before welcomed her.

"A bit wet out there this morning eh?"

"A tad." She shook her umbrella standing by the front window. "Well, I found out he's not having an affair. But I'll be looking for another job if he sees what I have done with this envelope."

"Don't worry, we sell those." The skinny young man in the white tee shirt held one up and waved it in the air. "See?"

"I'll take one!"

Shelby carefully slid the contents from the damp white envelope and slid them in the new white envelope.

"Perfect!" Exclaimed Shebly, "Just perfect. No one will ever know what a klutz I am."

As she handed the envelope to the boy behind the counter she blurted out, "See you!" Smiled then let herself out the front door.

"Happy girl." He mumbled.

Mayla walked through the front door of the law firm she glanced at Julia and grabbed her messages from the message box.

"Has Tom arrived?"

"He's waiting for you in the conference room along with Mr. Riley. You are late."

Mayla was not in the mood for Julia's smart comments after battling traffic to get to the office she snipped at Julia.

"Really Julia? Thank you. You are very observant."

Mayla rolled her eyes at Julia as she passed her by. "Brat."

"Good morning Mr. Riley. I'm sorry I was late this traffic, this weather, it's horrible. Please accept my apology."

Mr. Riley is a very mild mannered man. He sat with his hands folded on top of the conference room table. He had a Mr. Rogers way about him with his blue eyes and short graying hair.

"Oh don't worry. It took me over a half an hour to get here myself. We only have another month or so of this rain."

Tom and Mayla cannot understand how this man could rob insurance companies of over ten million dollars.

"Mr. Riley." Tom asked as Mayla sat down next to him. "We need to know what you have done with all of the money you have stolen. I am your attorney; you need to be open with me. It's the only way I can defend you."

Mr. Riley continued to sit with his hand folded in front of him. He sat up straight. Mayla began to feel guilty as she saw the pressure Tom was putting on Mr. Riley.

"I feel like you're not telling me something. Don't drag me into the courtroom only for me to find out the prosecution has something on you that we don't. Don't make me look like a fool Paul!"

"I've told you everything. We took vacations. We spared nothing! We drank the best wines, had massages, facials for my wife. Look at my passport. We traveled quite often."

"Mr. Riley, please," Tom was beginning to get agitated. "I know you're not telling me everything. Where is the money?"

Mayla flashed an evil look at Tom as she shrugged her shoulders and shook her head then spoke to Mr. Riley, "Please Paul, I don't think you understand. Once we get into the courtroom, if you have held back the tiniest bit of information, the prosecution will find it and you will go to jail for a very, very long time."

"I told you we."

Tom slammed his fist on the long cherry wood conference table.

"Tom! Please." Mayla was stunned.

"Well Mayla he is not telling the fucking truth and I will not look like a first year graduate in front of my peers! I don't want this case! I don't give a damn who paid for who to go to college! I want out! I will not represent this man!"

Tom walked towards the front door to leave as Mayla starred at his back.

Mr. Riley sunk in the leather chair with guilt. He put his hands over his eyes and spoke, "I've lost it. I have lost it all."

Tom dove in towards him as if he were listening to Jesus speak before he was crucified. "How did you lose ten million dollars Mr. Riley?"

"I took a bad gamble. I sent it over seas to Cuba. It was supposed to help oust Castro. To get rid of him and the communist party. He has caused so much heartache for so many families in South Florida including mine. So many people have died trying to get here to America."

Tom stopped at the door and turned to listen as Mayla breathed a sigh a relief.

"Yes everyone in this state ridicules these people but it is a horrible life they live. There is so much poverty and unhappiness. If you are not one of Castro's you will be living in hell. No food. Houses without plumbing. Rats in the streets. They will eat what little food you have. It's terrible"

"Why has it taken you so long to come clean with this story?"

"Please. Who and the hell would believe something like that?"

"Continue and let me be the judge." Tom waved his hand for Paul to tell more of his story.

"My wife is Cuban." Mr. Riley continued, "My wife and I met while I was on vacation in Venezuela. I was shopping in a small art store on the Island of Margarita where we both spotted a sculpture of a little boy. We fought over it. I won. She could not afford the price they were asking. I felt terrible. I asked her to dinner to reciprocate. We married in Argentina only two weeks later. To this day she tells her friends that the only reason she married me is so that she can look at this sculpture every day. She's such a beautiful woman."

"That's a lovely story." Mayla smiled.

Tom stood nearby with his hand on hip.

"She told me all the horrible things that were happening to her family in Cuba. She said she was lucky compared to most. At first I thought maybe she was marrying me to get out of Cuba. I was wrong. She left her family there. Her mother passed away a few years ago. She hadn't seen her since she left for her vacation in Argentina. She could have fought to get them over here but she didn't. Her brother wanted to stay to fight against communism over there."

"I see." Tom listened intently while Mayla took notes.

"My wife's brother was recently murdered by Castro. They tried to make it look like an accident, but the autopsy had proven it to be a murder. A murder with no suspects."

Tom raised his eyebrows and sat in front of Paul Riley.

Paul Riley stretched and then began to speak more. "My wife is having such a difficult time dealing with his death. She somehow feels responsible. They must not have been able to trace who sent the money because I am still alive. If this goes public, my family's life is on the line."

"Wow." Mayla sat back in her chair and drew her attention towards Tom. "Can you prove this?"

"All I have is an obituary. I am guilty. I'd rather sit in jail than put my family at risk. I'll do hard time if it means my family will be safe."

"We can get the jury to feel sorry for you. We will get your wife to testify and we will subpoena wire records from the bank."

"I don't think you understand Tom." Mr. Riley looked Tom in the eyes. "Castro has wiped everything clean. There is nothing left to prove that I have sent money down there, besides, I don't want to risk my family's life."

"They won't be, Castro or the Cuban government won't touch you. They don't need any negative publicity."

"Mayla, I want you to get as many Cuban immigrants who have personally experience the wrath of Castro first hand. I want families who have lost loved ones on their journey to a free country. I want stories. I need you to act like and investigative reporter from channel seven. Mr. Riley, why didn't you tell me sooner? We go to trial in two weeks?"

"Please Tom, who would believe such a story?"

"All of South Florida that's who."

Tom sat down in his chair and felt as if this case was finally going to go somewhere. Hopefully most of the jurors that will be picked are from a third world country. We may just get a lesser sentence for sympathy. For a man that loves his wife so much he would go to any lengths to pay back the man that brought her family so much hurt. We can do this Tom thought.

After the meeting Mr. Riley had been emotionally drained. He went home to his wife.

Tom invited Michael into his office for some good news.

"Michael would you care for a little afternoon celebration cocktail?"

"How's that?" Michael asked.

"We got Mr. Riley to speak."

Michael looked puzzled. "I don't understand."

"I actually feel sorry for the guy." Reaching for crystal glasses that sat in his credenza. "Here, this is my favorite whiskey."

"Thank you Tom, but could you please be more detailed for me?"

"It has a Castro link. Do you have any idea the publicity we will receive for this? We can get the jury on sympathy!"

"What and the hell are you talking about?"

You could see glimmer in Michael's eyes. "You make no sense."

"All the money was wired to a member of Mr. Riley's wife's family. They were trying to eliminate the Cuban government."

"Come on." Michael said as he crossed his legs and threw his hand towards Tom. "How can you prove such a story?"

"We will have his wife testify and Mayla is going to contact some of the local news stations to see if they can help her with some past stories of rafters that did not make it. It will be a total sympathy case. The prosecution can't go to Cuba to subpoena anyone over there. We finally have something to go on."

"Why did it take so long for him to tell his story?"

"He was in fear that something might happen to his family. What could possibly happen?" Tom tossed his hands to the air as if he just won first place in a relay race. "I bet we can get him less than ten years, or maybe just a light case of tax evasion. This case will make us famous!"

Michael smiled with relief. This case has caused him many sleepless nights. With Max and Philipo breathing down the back of his neck from New York.

"I certainly hope this case is as good as you think. If Mr. Riley is telling the truth Tom, you are right, we could get the best advertisement anyone could ever ask for. Your name will be plastered all over the state of Florida. You may even get a second interview on the Today Show."

"Hey, with all the publicity, I may just defend the next."

"Don't even say his name Tom." Michael interrupted.

"Have you heard there is a depression in the Atlantic?" Tom looked into his glass and sipped his whiskey then smacked his lips.

"Since when?" Michael asked.

"I heard it on the news this morning. I think this must be the seventh one this year. The hurricane center was predicting a light year for hurricanes. I guess they were wrong."

"We certainly don't need another Andrew. I'm still in court with a contractor who made off with someone's insurance money. I can't stand the guy."

"Now Michael, he pays you a great deal of money, isn't that why we do what we do?"

"I suppose so."

"Cheers!"

"Cheers."

CHAPTER NINE

Shelby and Mayla met for lunch at the small pizza place that over looked the New River at Riverfront where they would frequent happy hour. The aroma of basil and oregano filled the air.

"So are you excited?"

"Are you kidding Mayla?"

"I knew Michael would let you go. What are you going to have for lunch?"

"I think I'm going to have a slice of cheese with artichoke hearts."

"Sounds good. Now we need to talk about your trip! Make sure you pack condoms young lady!"

"Oh please Mayla." Shelby said as she gave Mayla a look of disgust, "I would never leave home without them!"

"Just be careful. Have you been to his house yet?"

"No not yet. He lives in North Miami Beach. He usually comes to see me."

"That's nice. I wonder what his house looks like."

"Oh I'm sure it's nice. I bet he has a maid."

"With that kind of money, of course he does."

"I could deal with that."

"I know you could."

Mayla looked up at the waitress that donned an earring in her nose. She looked like the typical twenty-year-old in Ft. Lauderdale. Tall and thin with bleach blond hair. A tattoo just above her bottom that she proudly showed by wearing very low cut shorts. Looks like she hasn't slept in three days. "I'd like a slice of cheese with artichokes and a coke."

"Make that two." Shelby joined in, "But cook mine well."

The anorexic waitress took the menus as she rolled her eyes at Shelby and walked off.

"I saw that!" Shelby blurted. The waitress continued her journey to the kitchen not looking back.

"You really need to be careful what you say to these people Shelby, she may spit on our pizza."

"She needs manners. I can't believe the way some of these people act. Maybe she had a run in with one of the boys from the mailroom. Maybe she's the pregnant one. Little bitch."

"No, I think the boys actually have better taste than that."

"Maybe."

When the pizza arrived Mayla examined hers very carefully lifting the cheese and flipping the artichokes from side to side.

"Mayla, I'm sure it's fine." Shelby said as she took a bite of her pizza.

"How can you be so calm?"

"My insides are jumping up and down. I promise. I'll be seeing Robert tonight. I don't know why I'm eating pizza now. We're going to a pizza place up in Delray."

"Delray? For pizza? Isn't that kinda far?"

"He swears by it. Apparently the wine selection is incredible."

"It's all about the wine isn't it."

"They say it makes the meal, or in some cases it makes the man."

"Sure, if they're ugly." Mayla giggled and sipped her Coke.

"So are you going to be a bad girl and sleep with him tonight?"

"I don't think so. This is the hardest thing I've ever had to do. I want him so badly Mayla I can hardly control myself."

"Why are you waiting? It's so unlike you, you little hussy."

"That's not a nice thing to say Mayla."

"I'm teasing you. Besides, if you do like him, you need to wait. Make it special, make it romantic. Your first night together. In London. You will be making love to the chiming of Big Ben."

"I certainly don't have a problem with that Mayla."

"No I guess I wouldn't either. You're so lucky Shelby, I wish I had someone who would excite me like that." Mayla put her head down to examine the crust of her pizza. It was almost as if she was pouting.

"Mayla? Are you sad?"

"No, I sometimes wish I had someone that I could depend on with little things around the house. This remodeling thing is beating me up. It would be fun to have some input. Maybe I'm changing. I never used to feel lonely or anything. Just lately I, it must be the remodeling."

"Hey, there's always Tom."

"Please Shelby."

"What's the big deal? On a serious note Mayla, Tom really is a great guy. I think that with the right woman he would make a great catch. I would guess that his machoism is nothing less than a show."

"Maybe. But I would have a hard time dating my boss."

"Excuse me." Shelby flagged the waitress; "May we have our check please? Get with it girl, so many romances start in the office. It's where you really get to know someone."

"Yes." Replied Mayla as she reached for her wallet, "And I don't want to lose my job. You know how I feel about that stuff. Look at how many sexual harassment cases we have had in the last year alone!"

"We're not a huge Fortune 500 corporation Mayla. You have nothing to worry about. Let's get back. I have much to do before my trip."

On the return to the office the heavens opened up and showed the love they had for Mayla and Shelby. Laughing through the rain as they ran towards the spinning glass doors to the entrance of the tall office building that graced a security guard named Waldo.

"Ladies? You're soaking wet! Wipe your feet, I don't want you to slip on the marble."

Waldo is an older gentleman in his late sixties. He is a balding man with gracious blue eyes. His wife always packs his lunch made from left over's from the night before. Waldo held up his sandwich and smiled at the girls. "Meatloaf."

"Has the investigation on the robbery turned up anything Mayla? Michael hasn't said anything to me."

"Nope, haven't heard a word. I'd like to know who invaded my privacy though."

The rain continued to fall throughout the day leaving a foggy mist in the air. Mayla sat with her head to her computer while Tom was on a conference call with a client. Michael cooed on his telephone with his newly rekindle marriage to Marlene and Shelby dreamt about spending the evening with Robert.

"Mayla?" It was Tom calling her from his office phone. "Can I see you for a minute?"

Mayla immediately stood to her feet and straightened her skirt, smacked her lips.

"Yes?" Mayla stood in the doorway and directed her eyes towards Tom. It was the first time she had ever thought of Tom in another manner other than her boss or someone to hang around with after work or on the weekends. Her stare deepened as she studied what he was wearing. A crisp white Ralph Lauren shirt and an Armani tie that matched his navy blue trousers. His office smelled like him. A scent she had never notice before. "What is happening to me?" She asked herself. "Why am I looking at him in a different light? Am I beginning to think he's attractive? Look at how those trousers fit him." Mayla's mouth slowly began to open as she was discovering a Tom she had never known before. His shoulders are so broad. His eyes held much character with traces of crow's feet. His hands are tan and muscular. Is this Tom? My boss? Could Shelby be right about him? Or has she put these thoughts in her head? "It is time for my period?" She thought to herself.

"Mayla?" asked Tom.

"Mayla are you alright?"

Mayla did not answer until Tom waved his hand in front of her eyes. He drew closer to her and spoke, "are you doing okay?"

"I'm sorry, my attention was on your chairs." She shook her head.

"What do you mean?"

"The fabric. I like the fabric. The color anyway. What is it that you need Tom?" Mayla replied as she felt as if she was caught with her hand in the cookie jar.

"I need to see what you have gathered so far for the case. Did you find me any people who are willing to testify?"

"I sure have." Replied Mayla with confidence. "I can print you out a report of the people who are willing to get on the stand in this case. They are mostly stories of the rafters. They have much better lives now here in America. They seem to be very willing to share their story with whoever wants to listen. I also have the Brothers to the Rescue leader to testify. If you remember they had a plane that was shot down by Castro about four years back. The Cuban community will be very supportive of Mr. Riley. I'm sure they will be picketing outside the courthouse showing their support for Mr. Riley during the trial."

"That's great."

"Thanks," She stood holding the door frame, "Don't worry Tom, I will make sure you get the publicity you want. Just make sure you wear that tie with those slacks, you look great!"

Mayla turned her back as her faced turned several shades of red. Embarrassed to ever have said something so forward. "Oh my." She thought to herself.

"Mayla?" Tom asked without questioning her innuendo, "May I have that paper today?"

Tom sensed that Mayla's remark was more than just a simple compliment, as she never gave him one.

"Yes I'll bring it to you."

Their eyes met before Mayla's shyness broke the curious stare. Tom fiddled with his white ceramic coffee cup as she passed though his office door. At the same time he felt a tinge of embarrassment as she may actually be responding to his continual egotistical passes.

That evening as the rain pounded down on the patio of Michael's home.

"Looks like we may never see the golf course again honey." Michael said to Marlene as he sipped his Merlot standing in front of his window. "Maybe we should think about going somewhere else to play."

"Are you taking me on a romantic golf vacation?" Marlene asked as she walked towards Michael and hugged him from behind. "Michael, what has happened to you? Lately you have been so invigorating. I find myself missing you during the day. I am growing to love you more and more. Are you sure you're not having an affair."

Michael chuckled as he turned around to face Marlene. "Never."

"Well honey, you know sometimes, when there's an affair the guilty party showers the poor unsuspecting spouse with love and attention."

"Marlene, honey, listen to me. Never."

"I see."

"I haven't been the greatest in the past few weeks. And I know you don't like to talk about it but it's the Riley case."

"What about the Riley case?"

"Well first it had to do with being thrown between Max and Tom. I really don't think they care for each other. They always put on a show like they're in a testosterone ring. I don't understand it."

"I don't know why you have to be the mediator."

"I always am. Besides, you know I'm good at that."

"Yes I suppose you are." She snuggled the small of his back.

"Then, I've learned how terrible life would be without you in it. Maybe someday you will meet Paul Riley. I feel bad for him. He has such a deep love for his wife. We finally find out the truth behind his story. It's quite sad."

"What is it?" Marlene showed concern.

"Mr. Riley's wife is Cuban. With all the money he embezzled from the insurance companies he apparently used it to over throw the Cuban government. It didn't work."

"Why get involved with such a mess?"

"Mrs. Riley's brother was killed by Castro and his men."

"That's terrible. Poor woman."

"It's very sad." Michael said, "His wife was devastated. She felt responsible for her brother's death. So Paul Riley tried to seek vengeance."

"Would you do that for me?" Asked Marlene as she stood on her tip-toes to whisper in Michael's ear.

"Absolutely. I would do anything for my true love." Michael turned to kiss Marlene's welcoming lips, "Where are the girls?"

"In bed."

"Hmm." Michael hummed as he pulled her close. "Here, now. Let me have you."

Michael slowly moved his hands around Marlene where he began to unbutton her white silk blouse. His mouth slid graciously down her neck onto her small round breast as he unlatched each button one by one. They fell to their knees without parting lips. Michael pushed his body onto hers. The rain fell harder and harder to camouflage the noise of satisfaction that Marlene was making. Michael found himself more and more excited as Marlene became more engulfed in her desire to orgasm. The bolts of lightning reflected off their naked bodies as they climaxed together. As they lie recovering on the cold marble floor taking deep breaths of satisfaction Marlene turned to Michael and explains how she has worked up an appetite.

"I'm so very hungry."

"Then I shall feed you my sweet love."

Michael lifted himself from the floor and turned to grab Marlene's hand.

"I must first excuse myself to the restroom."

Upon Michael's return from the restroom a sweet silhouette caught his eye in the kitchen. It was Marlene hunting for food.

As Marlene curved her spine to look in the refrigerator Michael found her voluptuous hips calling him again. Her skin was pale. She could have been a model for any Italian painter. Michael snuggled against her bottom reaching for her breasts. She was hard from the cold air. And so again, next to the refrigerator on the floor with the door open where the small light bulb of the refrigerator was their only audience.

The doorbell rang as Shelby ran down the stairs. It is Robert. Always prompt.

"It's raining!" She smiled as she opened the door, "and you are soaking wet! Come in. I will get you a towel so you can dry off!"

Shelby looked outside as she held the door open for him.

"Robert, this weather is awful. Maybe we should stay in. I don't mind. The pizza can wait for some other time. I have a great bottle of Cabernet and some Brie. We can put together a puzzle or play a game of strip poker."

"I would like to take you up on that offer Miss Peterson."

"Which one?"

"Let's start with the wine."

"Take your shirt off Robert."

"I'm sorry?" Robert found himself dumbfounded and somewhat nervous. "But we haven't even had any wine yet."

"I will dry it for you. The wine is in the wine rack in the kitchen. If you would open it, I will dry your shirt."

"Very well then."

Robert began to unbutton his white Ralph Lauren shirt. He was left standing in a white v-neck T-shirt where his salt and pepper chest hair peeped through.

"I'll get this right back to you."

After tossing Robert's shirt in the dryer, Shelby lit all of the ivory pillar candles she has scattered throughout her living room. A scene perhaps a little too romantic for a game of Battle Ship.

Robert carefully made his way into the living room with the opened bottle of Cabernet and two wineglasses.

"My this is nice. If I were a bit more forward I would say to skip the strip poker."

"We'll be playing Battle Ship." Replied Shelby as she invited Robert to sit down on her sofa.

"I would like to propose a toast." Robert held up his glass, "To a wonderful trip to London."

Shelby held her glass up to Roberts.

"To London."

Robert sipped his wine; "This is very nice. Robust. A bit peppery yet palatable."

What and the hell is he talking about? Pepper in wine?

"I'm assuming you approve."

"It's so wonderful I can hardly wait to take another taste. Just like I can hardly wait to make love to you for the first time. I hope I am not being to presumptuous, but I think you feel the same."

"Yes Robert," Shelby blushed, "I feel the same. Just don't disappoint me."

"I hope I won't."

"I doubt you will."

"To our first time." Again Robert raised his glass. "Are you looking forward to our trip? Have you packed?"

"I'm almost ready."

"Good. It will be nice to escape this rain. I'm not sure London will be much different, but God willing we will only have to suffer through a drizzle and not this tropical depression that we are experiencing now."

"I hope so." Shelby said as she set up her ships for the game. "By the way, I'm going to kick your ass in this game."

"Do I hear a wager?"

"I will only bet one dollar or I will make you dinner. How about you?"

Shelby was flirting heavily with her eyes as she leaned in towards Robert. His brown eyes stared down upon her as he gripped her arm.

"I tell you what. If I win, you make me dinner and I want the dollar. If you win, I will take you on my next London trip."

"That's a deal. Shake on it?"

"I think we can do much better than that."

Robert slowly leaned in towards Shelby to kiss her. She graciously accepted and did not let him part from her lips to quickly as she carefully slid her tongue into his mouth. Smiling as he pulled away Robert said, "I can't wait for more."

The rain had let up a bit when he was leaving to go home.

"The roads maybe flooded Robert, if you would like it's a long drive to North Miami, you can stay here."

"Thank you for the offer Shelby. But I really must go. I'm afraid I may not control myself if I stay. You do realize the next time I see you we will be on our way to London."

Robert stood up and walked towards the front door as Shelby followed.

"Yes. I know that."

"Be ready. The driver will be here at five."

"I'll be ready at four."

"Good night."

They kissed in the drizzling rain under the front porch light not worried about what any passers by may think.

"Night." Shelby said and closed the door behind her.

It was eleven o'clock not too late to call Mayla and gush to her about Robert.

"Mayla? Are you sleeping? Did I call too late?" Shelby said as she blew out her candles.

"No, I'm just watching the news. The weatherman is saying there is another storm following the tropical depression we are having now. They are saying it may turn into a hurricane. That means it's party time!"

"Where is it?"

"Far. It's somewhere around Jamaica. The winds are at thirty mile per hour. Not too bad. We'll have to plan a party Shelby!"

"I won't be here!" Plopping herself on the sofa and snuggling a pillow. "I'll be with Robert in London as we stroll down the cobble stone streets holding hands."

"That's right. London! Well, it will probably miss us anyway. How did it go tonight with Robert?"

"Mayla, older men are so different. He is so genuine. He is such a gentleman. With him there are no games. I don't feel like I have to try too hard to impress him. It's great, I can't explain it."

"Well maybe one day I will get to spend some time with an older man and we can share stories. I guess he went home."

"He just left."

"Wow Shelby I'm impressed! You're holding out! Did you at least blow him?"

"Mayla!"

"Well did you?"

"I behaved." Shelby paused, "I swear."

"Shelby, I think you put some crazy ideas in my head about Tom." You could hear the hesitation in Mayla's voice.

"What crazy ideas are you talking about?"

"Today he called me into his office. I looked at him differently, almost as if I was having a fantasy about him. I felt like he knew that I was checking him out."

"How could he possibly?"

"His face turned red Shelby. He wasn't his usual mouthy self."

"Just remember Mayla, you don't date within the office. It's not good for company moral." Shelby sounded as if she were scolding Mayla.

"Ya ya ya."

The rest of the week flew quickly at the firm although the dismal rain has not ended. Tom and Mayla worked diligently on the Riley case finding more Cuban Americans to testify keeping their evenings to themselves. Michael continued to romance Marlene with nights of untold pleasure. And Shelby finished packing for her trip to London with Robert.

CHAPTER TEN

"Good Morning Tom, I brought you a coffee from Starbucks." Mayla said as she walked into Tom's office on Thursday morning, "I thought you may need it since we'll be working our asses off today."

Mayla sat on the corner of Tom's desk after handing him the coffee. "This rain is going to drive me up the wall." Looking out the window that over looked the New River, "They say this storm headed our way is a tropical storm. That means the winds can reach up to fifty miles an hour. Then it may turn into a hurricane. I would say let's have a party but."

"But what?" Tom asked as he sipped his Starbucks coffee.

"Who would come?"

"I bet half the office."

"I doubt it. They'll be having their own party. Who'd want to hang with you after hours." She sipped her coffee throwing him a sly look.

"You."

"Pa-lease."

"Pa-lease? You'd stay if I asked."

"Only because you don't live in an evacuation area."

"Mayla, you'd stay. I'm Brad Pitt's look-a-like."

"I don't see the resemblance."

"You need to take the afternoon off."

"Where did that come from?"

"Take the afternoon off so you can get your eyes examined. I have a friend that's an optometrist."

"Funny Tom." She drank more of her coffee. He sat behind his desk admiring her legs.

"I hope Shelby has done something with her house. If she goes to London without putting up shutters she may come back and be homeless."

"If this thing hits like Andrew did in ninety-two, I'll make a killing."

"I would have a hard time defending slime that can kick somebody when they're down Tom. What if your mother lost her house and some ass of a contractor offered to fix her home and ran off with all the insurance money? I know it wouldn't make you too happy."

"I don't think we'll see too much of that this time Mayla, besides you work for me, so if I'm so terrible, so are you." Tom sipped his coffee and held his cup up, "This is great coffee. Thanks for thinking about me." He smiled as his eyes move in her direction. Mayla felt his eyes on her. She hesitated to look towards him to avoid a confrontation of eyes that may embarrass him or even worse yet, her. She put her head down and said "My pleasure."

Tom quickly changed the subject as he saw Mayla's shyness shine is her body gestures.

"Is Shelby ready for her trip?"

"I believe so. She took the entire day off so she could sleep in and enjoy her first moments over there. She leaves tonight around eight and arrives in London around seven in the morning."

Mayla began to fiddle with the trinkets on Tom's desk.

"You know Tom? I haven't even met Robert. Have you?"

"I think I met him at happy hour the night she met him. I barely remember him though. Too many cocktails."

He fiddled with his cup and took anther sip.

"I would have liked to have met him before they went away."

"Why?"

"To see if he measures up."

"Measures up to what? Are you jealous Mayla?"

Mayla's mouth opened wide as her face lit up with disbelief; "You have got to be kidding! Jealous of what?"

Tom shook his head. "She's got herself a successful, good looking, attentive and charming gentleman."

"And I am very happy for her."

"You could have one too."

"Who?" She questioned Tom.

"Who do you think?"

"You, no doubt."

"I knew you were a smart girl."

"Tom?" a voice came over the speaker phone, "Is Mayla in there?"

"Yes, I'm in here." Mayla responded with annoyance, as she didn't want her conversation to be interrupted with Tom.

"It's Shelby."

"Put her through here please." She spoke loudly.

The phone beeped as Mayla picked up the handset, "Well are you ready to go?"

"Yes, but I forgot to deliver an envelope for Michael. He'll kill me if he ever finds out."

"Do you want me to do it for you?"

"Yes please Mayla. It's in my desk drawer on the right hand side. I've been so caught up in the excitement of this trip that it slipped my mind. Please don't tell Michael or Tom I had forgotten about this."

"No problem. What is the address?"

Mayla wrote down the address that the envelope was to be delivered to on a sticky note and put it in her pocket.

"Can you do this for me right away?"

"Yes I will."

Mayla hung up the phone and turned to Tom.

"Okay, she's a little excited. She's forgetting things."

"Excited for her trip?"

"I guess so. Enjoy your coffee Tom."

When Mayla turned towards the door, she left her sweet florally scent of Carolina Herrara behind.

Tom watched her in slow motion as if he were a movie handler.

"Maybe." He thought.

Mayla proceeded to Shelby's office. Shelby had decorated her office with pictures of her family of whom she was very close to. There was a picture of her with friends from college standing on the side of a bar with their heavy mugs of green beer raised in the air. Shelby was wearing a leprechaun hat. Mayla scrambled through her desk looking for the envelope she had forgotten to deliver for Michael. No one ever questioned his reasoning for wanting delivery of these large white envelopes after they discovered he was not having an affair.

"Ooh, chocolates my favorite." Mayla's eyes lit up as she opened one of Shelby's drawers. "I'll have to have just one." She picked the chocolate. They were one of those fancy Swiss chocolates bottle with a liquid center cleverly wrapped in foil. Michael would bring them in for Shelby as she would sometimes stay late and help with paperwork. Mayla found the envelope where Shelby promised it would be. After studying its pretty wrap, Mayla couldn't wait to rip back the foil that surrounds this delectable creamy little morsel from Switzerland. With the envelope under her right arm she gently peeled the foil from the chocolate shaped bottle treating it if it were a fragile newborn baby. Not wanting to devour the entire chocolate at once, she brought it close to her mouth as she snipped the top half of the chocolate shaped bottle with her perfectly straight white teeth. It happened almost in slow motion as the liquid center drizzled down her chin onto her light blue silk blouse.

"Shit." Mayla said as she licked the sweet cherry flavored liquor from her lower lip. Tom stood in his doorway amused with Mayla as she acted like a child swimming in a sweet creamy pool of chocolate. She ran to her office to put the envelope down not noticing Tom's presence. After unsuccessfully trying to clean her blouse with a tissue she resorted to the restroom where she spent the next fifteen minutes with soap and paper towels. It was a new blouse.

"Maybe the cleaners can help."

The envelope sat unattended on Mayla's desk as her emergency occupied her and distracted her for the rest of the day. It would remain there helpless and forgotten as piles of paperwork from the Riley case overtook it.

Shelby had her bags neatly stacked by the front door waiting for the limousine driver. The big dark green suitcase she packed carried some of her favorite outfits including what her and Mayla bought while shopping at Victoria's Secret in the Galleria Mall. In the smaller brown leather bag that she usually brought when she traveled had chocolate chip cookies, her black cashmere sweater and a book. The only time she had to read was when she flew.

The anticipation for the departure of her home grew as she paced back and forth in front of the mirror that hung next to the front door. She would occasionally stop and look at her eyes making sure a piece of black mascara did not fall and smudge her face.

She reflected on her childhood as she flipped through her hair searching for grays. When she was younger she recalls telling her mother that she was going to marry when she was sixteen. She was eight years old at the time. Her mother answered her that she would do no such thing. She wanted to plan her wedding so badly, she remembers writing a list of all the relatives that she would invite. All of her aunts and uncles were on the list. She tried to recall if she invited any of her friends. It was so important to her, this wedding of hers. *Maybe now.*

Time was creeping by slowly as Shelby was just short of wearing a hole in the rug.

"Mom." Shelby stopped pacing; "I should call my Mom." She began to pace again. "I can't. Not now. I'm too nervous and she'll make me feel even more out of control. I know," Shelby paused, "I'll have a glass of wine. Just a sip. That will help me." As Shelby turned toward the kitchen the doorbell chimed. It was so much louder than she ever remembered. It was almost as if it stopped time. She stopped as she felt excitement rush through her body. It's time! Shelby took a deep breath as she opened the front door to greet the younger Spanish man standing there in a black suit. His eyes were dark brown. His hair was slicked backed into a curl ponytail.

Wow. What a ham.

"Hi." She smiled.

"Good afternoon Miss Peterson, my name is Armando, may I take your bags?" His tongue twisted and turned, as his accent was thick.

"Certainly. Here they are." Shelby pointed to her bags then turned to look around her townhouse before she jetted off to London. Her thoughts occupied herself as she sat in the back of the big black limousine. The limo was new. The leather scent surrounded her. "I feel like a princess." She softly spoke to herself. Secretly wishing one of her ex-boyfriends would see her being stolen from America by a handsome man. "I can't believe this is happening to me." Shelby reflected on her hurtful relationships from the past. *So this is what it's all about. Falling in love.* She finally got the respect from a man that she craved. Her hurtful relationships from the past would slowly disapate. She succumbed to the reasoning for them. It was so she would appreciate Robert and the way he treated her. Shelby's mind began to run wild as she pictured herself with Robert in one of the parks of London that adorned beautiful lush gardens and tall marble statues. They were sitting on the soft green grass enjoying finger sized Brie sandwiches they bought from Harrods deli on the first floor. They were talking, laughing and pointing at the sky. Sharing secrets. Making love with their clothes on. Not touching. Falling in love. Shelby paused from her dream to see the traffic outside. It was rush hour. The expressions on people's face were pure anticipation and frustration. *Only one day left of work you poor people, then you will be off like me. But they will not be having as wonderful of a time as myself.* She began to drift back to her dream. Robert sat back on his left hand and touched Shelby's cheek with the other. "I love you," he said just as an airplane circled in the sky and released white smoke that scribbled "marry me."

Shelby's dream carried her all the way to the airport. The limousine slowed then came to a stop in front of the busy Delta terminal. The driver opened the door for her and carried her baggage to the man in the Delta uniform standing outside.

"Checking in your luggage out here Miss?"

"Yes please." Shelby said as she scrambled in her purse for a twenty-dollar bill to tip the driver.

"Oh no Miss." The handsome driver waved his hand, "That has been taken care of."

Shelby smiled and thanked Armando for getting her there safely in the rush hour traffic.

"Where will you be traveling to today?"

"London." It felt good to say that she thought.

"Okay Miss, you will have to check in inside the terminal. Have a nice flight."

Shelby smiled at the friendly Delta baggage handler as she turned toward the sliding doors and toted her green Travel Pro bag behind her.

When the doors opened she felt the cool air rush onto her blowing her blond hair in her eyes. She shook her head and brushed the hair away from her face as she continued to walk towards the ticket counter where she stood and waited for Robert to appear. As she waited she began to slip back into her dream. *I wonder how many children we'll have. I wonder if we will have children, does he want them? I wonder if I will move into his home in North Miami or if we'll build another. I wonder if he is as serious about me as I am beginning to feel for him.*

These were all questions that Shelby was hoping to find the answers to on her trip. There was noise in the background of her dream, *Mr. Lilly please meet your party at the Delta ticket counter.* Slipping back into her dream they were in a small restaurant in an alley with cobblestone streets. On the entrance there were two large flowerpots filled with colorful pansies. *Paging a Mr. Lilly, your party is waiting at the Delta ticket counter.* Her dream was interrupted as a tall gentleman stopped abruptly in front of her; he seemed out of breath, it was Robert.

"There you are!"

"Hi!" Shelby said as she was beaming.

"Are you ready?" asked Robert as he reached for Shelby's leather bag.

"Oh yes I am."

They kissed. Just a small peck on the lips.

"Great."

They stood in line for the next few minutes before reaching the counter where they checked in their bags.

The sun was slowing falling as Mayla peeled back her curtains from her bedroom window. Facing westward, it wasn't the most pleasant view in South Florida. It donned tall buildings from downtown and older condos in the surrounding area. Despite the heat there were rollerbladers skating feverishly before clouds blew over again. The street was settling from the rush hour traffic.

"I'm bored." She said. Thoughts swirled through her mind as she flirted with the idea of calling Tom.

"*Do it.*"

"*Are you crazy?*"

"*Do it anyway.*"

"*No.*"

"*Well if you don't, he will be on to you.*" The other voice in her head sang those words.

"*I can't. I'm the girl.*"

"*This is the twenty-first century girl, if you don't call him someone else will.*"

"He may think I'm being too aggressive if I call him. How could he? We never even held hands. But what if something really happens? It could be a good thing. Then again it could be horrible. He is my boss. Oh what the hell. As far as I'm concerned, we are still just friends. Or co-workers. Or employee-boss. Great. I'm asking my boss on a date. Wait, this is not a date. I just want to do something, something like we always have. We can see a movie or go rollerblading. That's it. I'll call to see if he wants to go rollerblading. I'll use this weather as an excuse."

She eventually ended the one-sided conversation with herself.

Mayla dialed Tom's number from her bedroom. She sat on her bed and looked in the mirror that was directly across from her on the dresser. She noticed her red splotchy face. She hung up the phone and paced around her bed.

"I shouldn't do this." She paused and looked in between the cracks of the blinds that guarded her window.

"It will be dark soon." Mayla quickly dialed Tom's number so she would not have time to change her mind.

"Hey baby. Can't stay away from me?" It was Tom. Mayla felt relief overcame her entire body as her red splotchy face turned to its normal olive coloring. Tom was comforting. He was acting like the idiot she had grown to like.

"Don't give yourself too much credit Tom."

"So tell me baby, what can I do for you?"

"Well baby," Mayla said with slight sarcasm, "It's a nice night and I thought you might want to take advantage of the weather. It's not raining."

"So how about a romantic walk on the beach? We can get a bottle of your favorite wine and."

"How about rollerblading?" Mayla interrupted.

"I can be over at your house in fifteen minutes."

Tom hung up the phone without saying goodbye.

Mayla raised her eyebrows as she placed the headset on the receiver, "Must be excited."

Tom was over in the fifteen minutes like he promised. Mayla never quite remembered seeing his legs before. They were skinny with light blond hair growing on them. She called him chicken legs and giggled as he entered her home.

"Chicken legs?"

"Yes. Chicken legs."

"Look at your ass in those spandex shorts."

"Huh?" Mayla turned to look at her bottom, "Are you saying it's big?" She looked upset.

"I never said that."

Mayla smiled and rolled her eyes, "So you approve."

After sharing a glass of water they went rollerblading along the beaches of Ft. Lauderdale. Although all night there was continual sexist remarks from Tom, he remained a gentleman skating on the outside near the traffic so no oncoming traffic would harm her.

The airplane pounced and screeched along the runway as it landed at London's Gatwick airport. The sky seemed a bit cloudy, as there was a slight mist to the morning air.

"It looks a bit chilly." Shelby said as she held Robert's hand to heart.

"Hmm, if we didn't pack well for this trip, it will be a good excuse to do some shopping."

Shelby smiled at Robert without saying a word. Robert took his hand from her heart and placed it on the back of her head as he leaned into kiss her.

"Tonight." He said as his lips parted from hers. "Tonight I will make love to you for the first time. That's if you will have me."

"I'll make love to you now Robert. Here on this airplane while we are bouncing down the runway with everyone surrounding us, hearing us and maybe even seeing us. I'll make you moan and maybe even scream. Everyone will think your precious ears are plugged and you are in pain and then just as the flight attendants rush to your aid, I will have finished you off. And you will have to excuse yourself to the smoking section my dear Robert even though you don't smoke."

A small bit of drool fell from the corner of Shelby's mouth as the plane pulled into the gate. *"Stop fantasizing."* She continued to talk to herself. *"One day you will have an orgasm right smack in the middle of the post office or grocery store because you let your mind get so carried away."*

"Your lips are wet Shelby." Robert wiped them with his thumb.

"Busted." Shelby said with confidence. "I was thinking about what you said. I can hardly wait."

The air was thick and damp. A bit of a chill in the air surrounded them. Robert took a deep breath.

"It may not be sunny, but I do love the air here."

Shelby stood close and held his left arm. Tilting her head and resting it on his shoulder. She sought comfort there. A comfortable comfort. A long awaited comfortable comfort. Lucky girl.

They drove through the countryside to the hotel. Even though it was fall, green grass and colorful flowers were everywhere. They barely spoke a word to each other as they admired the old stone homes. Some had been dated as far back as the early sixteen hundreds.

Lovely Shelby thought. Robert pointed out a woman fishing water from the well just outside her home. The drive was very serene.

They were staying at only a few blocks from Piccadilly. The hotel was small. It sat evenly in between other buildings. Some were hotels, others were businesses and the ones that had long flowerpots on their windowsill were homes. The wrought iron gate that surrounded the front of the hotel was covered in thick black paint.

The doorman that greeted them was sharply dressed in a navy blue jacket with tails and big gold buttons. He held the door open for people as they entered the hotel.

"Good day." said the man with the peculiar graying moustache that stood on ends. His English accent was prominent.

Shelby smiled at the man as she entered. Robert nodded, "Good day."

The small elevator with the gates took them to the third floor. The room was tiny. There was only one bed. It was a queen-sized bed with a floral printed duvet cover. A television was carefully hidden behind an armoire. The bathroom had white marble floors and its very own blown dryer. Helpful and accommodating when traveling in a foreign country. A variety of soaps sat near the sink.

Shelby lifted the soap from the silver dish and held it to her nose. She closed her eyes and devoured the scent. *Lemon verbena, my favorite.*

CHAPTER ELEVEN

"Good morning. Michael Devon speaking." Michael answered his phone Friday morning sitting at his desk in his office.

"Is it? Is it really a good morning?" The irate voice from the other end was Max. Michael sat back in his chair and rolled his eyes. Resting his head in his hand, *this is not the man I wanted to speak to, not today.*

"Here we go again." He sighed. *"This guy is going to have a heart attack."*

"Michael, I don't know who in hell you have delivering the envelopes off but it seems their curiosity had gotten the best of them."

"What are you talking about." He brushed his forehead as he looked out the window. The construction workers had taken a break from the building that was going up on the other side of the river.

"The information is not in the white envelope that I had instructed you to put them in. And in addition to the mishap, I sent a messenger to pick up the other envelope and it was not there!" Max's voice grew louder and as he became more fierce. "Perhaps you can tell me what and the hell is going on Michael? You assured me there would never be a problem! Now I have this to deal with? What kind of business are we trying to run? Do you have any idea what this can do to you, your family and the firm? Philipo will have my ass. Not to mention yours." Max's words caught Michael's attention as he sat up in his chair and felt his world sink around him. He began to feel flush and sick to his stomach.

"Max I."

"Michael," interrupted Max, "Find out who is meddling in company business. And find the other white envelope. I want it by Monday, and Michael," Max paused for what seemed to be an eternity, "you know what to do if this envelope has disappeared."

There was silence on the other end of the line. Michael dare not speak a word in fear Max may still be there. He gripped the phone tightly as the palm of his hands began to sweat not letting go until he heard a recording, "If you'd like to make a call please hand up and try." Michael hung up the phone, pushed his chair back and stood up and walked towards Shelby's office.

No wonder you never have a woman on your arm at any of our business dinners.

"It's got to be here somewhere." He said shuffling through Shelby's desk. Michael began to panic as he opened her drawers and found nothing. *"Where can it be? Shelby don't let me down."*

He continued his search looking frantically in the same places two and even three times. Throwing papers on top of her desk from side to side and looking in the trash can. He became frustrated. He became a wrinkled mess. After giving up, he sat down on Shelby's chair and nearly began to weep.

"Michael?" It was Mayla. She stood with curiosity on her face. "What's wrong? You look very upset."

"How can I get in touch with Shelby?"

"I don't have her number. She said she would call me when she arrived in London and give me the number to her hotel."

"I need it as soon as possible."

"Can I help you with something in the meantime?"

"No." Michael stood to his feet; "I just need the number to her hotel as soon as she calls you."

"Sure." Mayla responded as Michael walked past her.

As she turned to head back towards her office she ran smack into Julia the receptionist. Mayla felt like whacking her on the head as she gave her a dirty look. Not noticing the glare Mayla threw at her, Julia shouted like a bugle, "Hurricane is on its way! We need to get prepared!" Mayla walked into Tom's office around the corner where he was sitting at his desk working on his computer.

"Hey."

"Hey is for horses. What's up?" He looked up at her.

"The hurricane is heading our way? Have you heard that?"

"I certainly have."

"How far away is it?"

"Let's put it this way," Tom stretched and pointed at Mayla, "We will probably close the office early today so we can get to Home Depot for plywood to board up our houses and to Publix for food and water and batteries and ice." Tom rambled on.

"Wow! I had no idea it was that close!" Mayla began to pace, "I have hurricane shutters. I have tons of canned goods. But I live east of US1. They'll make me evacuate. What will I do?"

"You can stay with me." Tom began to flirt. "We can make margaritas or drink wine and have one of your gourmet dinners. We'll have our own little party as we listen to the news or soft romantic music on my portable radio. We can even build a tent in my living room. I'll make you feel safe Mayla."

"Can I bring Vermin?" She didn't hesitate to respond.

"And you're silky pajama's. And your teddy bear." Tom coyly added.

Mayla's tension began to ease. She knew she could spend her time with Tom even in the middle of a crisis and still laugh.

"When are you leaving? Don't you have to board up your house?"

"No. I have the fancy hurricane shutters. Press a button and presto, the whole house is locked up. Cheaper insurance." Tom was cocky as he looked at Mayla.

"Fine. I'm coming over then. I hope Shelby's house is going to be okay. There was only a tropical depression last we heard."

"It officially turned into a hurricane this morning. They said the winds are picking up quickly. They are expecting it to hit somewhere between Miami and West Palm Beach. Which leaves us in Ft. Lauderdale in the middle."

"Have you heard how strong the winds are yet?"

"Somewhere around seventy nine miles an hour. They're expected to strengthen." Tom began to talk with a more serious tone. "Look Mayla, don't worry. You have insurance. I live out west and you and Vermin are going to stay with me. Understand?"

"Understand." She replied.

"Very good then. As soon as we hear more we will more than likely close the office. You will go home and get your things and come to my house." Tom was excited to have her company. He will go home after work and dust his guest bedroom for her.

It was Friday night in London. The sky had just fallen to dusk leaving a misty air behind. Shelby and Robert were having dinner at Ophelia's not far from the Tower of London. The restaurant was very tiny. It had only a few scattered tables with ivory colored tablecloths. The ceiling was wallpaper with old sheet music. Candles sat glowing in the corners and Ophelia was the hostess, the waitress and the chef. She would sit and talk with her customers as they drank the wine she served. Afterwards they would sign their name to a registry she kept near the telephone in the back of the restaurant. It was obvious this was Ophelia's passion. To feed her patrons well and then make friends with them. She was a heavier set woman with long brown hair she kept tied behind the back of her head. Her English accent was thick yet not lady like. She was a woman who spoke her mind yet showed her love for music and her customers.

"All right?" Ophelia asked as she approached Robert and Shelby with a piece of white cardboard in her hands..

"I'm wonderful." Shelby said, as she looked back at her and smiled.

"Fine. Thank you." Robert added.

"Like to see the wine list?" asked Ophelia as she held up a laminate card with only a few wines gracing it.

"We would love to." Robert answered for the both of them.

"Very well here it is. I've got some great bottles in me cellar right now. Can't really recommend one particular one cause they're all so tasty."

Shelby scanned the menu even though she was not that hungry. Her excitement had filled up her stomach. *What would happen after dinner?*

"Everything looks so wonderful." She said

"Should I close my eyes and point my finger at one?" Robert asked as he looks at the woman with the brown hair.

"Might have to." Ophelia said in a more serious tone, "How bout me specials? Would ya like to hear em?"

"Let's be adventurous!" Shelby interrupted, "Ophelia will you order for us?"

"Great idea."

Ophelia brought pistachio encrusted salmon for Shelby and grilled lamb chops with a mint glaze for Robert.

"More wine?" asked Robert, "We've finished this bottle."

"Let's have another." She agreed.

"You know what they say, it's not the wine that makes the wine great, it's the company you are sharing the wine with."

Shelby smiled as she lifted her glass from the table. "To great company then." Their glasses clinked together.

The restaurant bared only two other tables with people. The small round table that sat near the front window had a young couple in they're twenties flirting heavily over their sorbet. It must have been their first or second date. The young girl was blushing as she leaned in to her date. He held her free hand and gushed. They were cute. Obviously never struck by the bug that can destroy a heart. It was new, and they were new at it. Sweet.

The larger table sat in the middle of the restaurant. It was a family of seven celebrating the gentleman's birthday that sat at the head of the table. His family made him wear a birthday hat. There was a colorful balloon tied to the back of his chair. They had finished eating his cake. Now he was opening gifts. His smile never left his face. That had to be his wife that sat next to him. She was pleased to see he was having a lovely birthday. She was a fair skinned woman with a bun on top of her head. An English lady is what most would refer her to. His children sat around the table admiring his gifts as he open them.

"I'm having such a wonderful time Robert. I can't thank you enough for inviting me to join you."

"I'm just glad you could make it." Replied Robert as poured another glass of wine for Shelby as he spoke, "Or else I would have to enjoy this dinner by myself."

"All right then you two. How was your dinner?" Ophelia asked as she wiped her hands on her apron. "Ready for some bread pudding?"

There was a pause as they looked at each other and shrugged.

"I think we should give it a try Robert."

"Well then I'll bring ya's a bread pudding with two spoons."

Ophelia returned with a trail of steam from the bread pudding following her. "Here we are. Enjoy. And please, I would like you to fill out my registry if you can keep your hands off each other." She said that without smiling.

Robert wiped his face with his napkin then placed his hands on his stomach.

"That was absolutely delicious!"

"Glad ya liked it. Here's your bill." Ophelia placed the check in front of Robert.

After paying the dinner bill and leaving Ophelia a gracious tip they returned to the hotel in a black taxi. Greeting the doorman as they walked in.

"Good evening."

"Good evening." Robert added as he turned to Shelby, "Care for a night cap?"

"Sure."

There was a small cherry wood bar in the lobby to the right of the front entrance. Liqueur was carefully lined up against the back of the bar. It was not a fully stocked bar. A few wines and liqueurs, you might be able to order a beer. No one was there except the bartender.

"Good evening. What can I get you?" Asked the young bartender with a pointy noise and white skin.

"I'll have an amaretto."

An amaretto used to be the drink of choice for Shelby when she was in college. She thought it made her look sophisticated. Yet she was able to handle the sweet almond going down without making a face. It was always an amaretto, besides all of the boys thought it tasted nice on her lips. Sweet. They would come back for more. She thought Robert would like it also.

"And I would like a frangelica." Added Robert, "Maybe we should bring these back to the room."

"What's the rush sailor?" She flirted.

"There is no rush. I have been waiting for a very long time Shelby. It's no secret we want to make love to each other."

"Well then, follow me." She made her move.

She hadn't been that forward in eons. Not since college she thought.

The elevator ride to the third floor seemed to take an eternity although they were kissing and groping each other and performing a balancing act with their drinks. As the elevator came to a stop on the third floor the doors opened Shelby grabbed Robert by the belt around his waist and tugged him towards the room. Desperately trying to find the paper key to the room, Robert spilled his drink over the front of Shelby's blouse.

He found the key in his left pant pocket and slid it into the lock.

"I can fix that." Robert said as he opened the door. He tossed his glass to the floor and took Shelby's drink from her hand. He placed it on the table the sat next to the window as he fumbled to kiss her neck then work his way to her blouse where he licked the sweet Frangelica off her.

"What a shame to have wasted such a drink." Shelby was begging for him to continue as she bent her neck back.

"I bet you taste just as good."

Working his way into her blouse with his mouth and using his fingers to undo the buttons. Shelby straightened her arms letting it fall to the floor. Not waiting for Robert to make the second move she stepped out of her shoes and reached for her back to unhook her black lacey bra from Victoria's Secret. Exposing herself without hesitation. He made her feel sexy. Almost as if she were a goddess.

"You're beautiful Shelby."

Robert caressed her breast as he put them in his mouth.

Shelby threw her head back as she looks towards the ceiling. The anticipation is over. As she pulled her skirt up, Robert slid her panties down her legs that were impatiently waiting to open. Robert barley unzipped his trousers before Shelby was tugging at him. Kissing his mouth then his throat. She could taste his cologne. How delightful. His scent made her want him more. Shelby pulled his boxer shorts to the floor and he stood erect with his white Polo shirt still in tact, she was now ready for him. Kissing her opened mouth and grabbing the back of her hair Robert found his way inside her. He continued to please her leaving his white Polo shirt on.

Lying breathless on the bed Robert turned to Shelby and began to stroke her blond tousled hair.

"I'm not through with you."

"I didn't think you would disappoint me." She was gasping for air. *Heaven. I'm in heaven.*

"I believe I am falling in love with you Shelby." He leaned towards her on his side propping his head with his hand.

As her eyes began to well up she spoke softly to him; "I am falling in love with you too."

"No," he said, "Listen to me. I know I love you."

"I love you too." She leaned to kiss his nose.

I can't believe this is happening to me. Shelby began talking to herself again. This could be the man I am going to marry. I feel something inside my heart I have never felt before. This must be what my mother is talking about. You'll know when it's right. She could hear her mother's voice as if she were sitting next to her.

Maybe she can make out those invitations now. Maybe mother will update that list I had asked her for so many years ago.

"I'm building a house in Boca, Shelby. I will be moving there in a month or so, depending on the contractors." Robert's tone was serious.

Her mind ran *again, "He wants me to move in with him. This is it! Where's the ring?"* Her heart began to pound not knowing how she will react to his next words. *"Will it be marriage? Will he ask to move in with me until his house is done?"*

"Tell me about it." Wow! *A house in Boca. . This must be going somewhere.*

"I was wondering if you knew a decorator." He stroked her hair some more.

"Me." She confessed she was serious. How would he respond? With an answer like that she was certain he would propose to her.

"Shelby," Robert propped himself up on his elbow facing towards her. "I am married."

"You're so funny." She said as she grabbed the pillow she was lying on and hit Robert on the head.

"Shelby, please." He seemed upset. "I am married. It's the truth. I did-n't know how to tell you. I had gotten so caught up in you. You tantalize me. I couldn't help myself. You excite me! I feel young again. I knew from the moment I met you I would fall in love with you."

Shock overcame her body as she could only lie there in disbelief. Not speaking a word she felt her whole world begin to crumble, her future, her dreams, they were just that. Dreams. Mother, I don't need that list anymore. A waste. A waste of her time. Her heart. What about my heart she thought. If this man had cared for me at all he would have left me alone. Finally anger slowly began to creep into her body. She felt as if she had caught on fire. First her stomach, than her heart. The fire began to burn her face and the rest of her body to her toes. Trying as hard as she could to remain like a lady and then in less than an instant, she surrendered to her anger.

"You bastard!" She stood to her feet and pulled the blankets off the bed to cover her vulnerable body. "How could you? How could you drag me here to London and tell me you are married? I thought you were for me! Forever! I gave myself to you, you lying bastard!" Shelby began to pound on his chest. "I'll call your wife! I'll tell her everything! I hate you!"

Robert stood still as she beat him knowing he deserved it. He did not try and stop her.

Tears flowed down her cheeks as she fumbled to find her clothes.

"Shelby, Please listen to me."

She put on her clothes as Robert stood only in his Polo shirt following her around the tiny room.

"No. There is no excuse or reason! You are a selfish man! You have done this only for yourself! You didn't think of me! You did not think of your wife! Just you! It's all about you Robert!"

Shelby couldn't believe that she was throwing such harsh words upon the man that she had made love to only moments earlier.

"Shelby. Please listen to me!" Robert raised his voice. "I am divorcing my wife. She agreed to let me stay with her until my home was finished! It's the truth! Please, you must believe me."

"Oh yes Robert, I really do believe you!" Her arms were whipping around her body, "And let me ask you something, does she know I exist?"

"No." Replied Robert as he looked to the ground. "I told her I would not peruse anyone while we were under the same roof."

"Is there anything else maybe you can surprise me with Robert? How many times have you been married? How many children do you have?"

"I have a daughter. Her name is Francis." Robert reached for Shelby trying to hug and hold her.

"You mother-fucker!" Pushing him away from her. "Wouldn't your family be happy to know you're in London fucking some blond bimbo! Get away from me!"

"Shelby please, you are not a bimbo! I love you!"

"What is her name?"

"Neddie." Robert stood like an ape with his hands directly by his side realizing he would not win this argument. He no longer looked like a confident powerful man that Shelby had thought him to be. But like a child that had been scolded by his parents for riding his bike in the middle of the street. After getting dressed she frantically began to pack her suitcase. Robert had only put his boxer shorts on as he continued to beg her to listen to him. She did not respond as she picked up the phone and calling the front desk.

"Yes, could you please connect me to Delta Airlines?" She turned her back to Robert and tried to fight the tears so she could speak with the airlines.

"My pleasure." The woman responded on the other end.

She was on hold.

"Shelby damn it listen to me!" Robert became angry as she ignored him. She was leaving and he could not stop her. She reached for her purse where she took out her credit card to pay the fee for changing her ticket. Her flight would be leaving at six o'clock in the morning. The tears had momentarily dried up.

She wished he would do something, say anything to make her stay. Tell her it was a lie. Is it April fools? No, I am the only fool here.

"Give me money for the taxi to the airport." Shelby demanded as she stood to her feet and held out her hand.

"I will not!" Robert declared hoping it would make her stay.

"Fine. I'll take a gosh damn cab and send you the bill." Grabbing her purse and suitcase she walk towards the door. "I'm telling your wife."

"I really wish you wouldn't do that."

"If I were you, I wouldn't go home." She began to threaten him. Her anger was like a giant steam train going down hill about to run over anything that stood in her way.

"Shelby. Please." He grabbed and held her arm as she stood by the front door, "don't call my house."

She squinted her eyes and shook her head. Pissed again.

"Deal with it."

Shelby left Robert sitting on the bed in his boxer shorts as she opened the front door. She really didn't want to leave him and had hoped he would chase her into the hall telling her it was all a lie or maybe he would wake her from this horrible nightmare she was having. As she stood by the elevator Robert did not flinch. The door to room 302 did not open and he did not chase after her nor did he wake her from her horrible dream. This was all too real. As the bell to the elevator rang and the doors opened they would take Shelby away from Robert maybe forever.

CHAPTER TWELVE

"Time to go." Michael said to Tom as he walked in his office. We have about twenty-four hours before the hurricane hits land. Make sure you turn down your computer and unplug it. I've already done the copiers and faxes."

"You can leave those on. I hate that damn fax machine."

"I told you to go with the Toshiba's fax Tom, but you had to try and get a date with that blond sales rep." Michael pointed at him as if he were scolding him. "You'll learn."

"Thank God I have hurricane shutters." Tom said ignoring Michael's comment.

"Does anyone know if Shelby's townhouse has shutters?"

"Might want to ask Mayla. She should know."

Tom dialed the phone to Mayla's office.

"Time to go. Get Vermin and some clothes for a few nights. You never know. Also, does Shelby have hurricane shutters?" He spoke to Mayla as he secured his office unplugging all of his small appliances including his stereo. *I thought this building was protected against surges.*

"I don't think so. She was talking about getting some at the beginning of the season but I don't think she ever did."

Tom signaled Michael that the answer was no. Michael waved and mouthed to Tom, "Stay in touch through the course of the storm."

Tom focused in on his conversation with Mayla, "Make sure you turn down and unplug your computer. Are you leaving now?"

"Yes in a few minutes. I'll call you as soon as I leave my house."

Mayla stood and looked around her office after unplugging her computer. Her eyes scanned her office looking for something that maybe important for her to bring home with her. There was nothing. She actually felt a tinge of excitement knowing she would be alone with Tom for at least a full day. She began to wonder what he would be like in his own environment. Alone with her. Would he bare his chest with her there in his house? Would he walk around in boxers? She turned off the light to her office and just as she closed the door, the phone began to ring. She did not hear it. It was Shelby. She left a Mayla a desperate message.

The drive to the airport was difficult. The driver would occasionally look in his rear view mirror to check on Shelby. He saw that she had been crying and was still upset nearly after thirty minutes into the ride.

"Not worth it, miss." He spoke looking at her in the rear view mirror.

"Sorry?"She wiped her face and looked to the mirror that she was about to have a conversation with.

"Not worth it I said."

"What's not worth it?"

"The man you're crying after."

Shelby didn't feel much like discussing what had just happened to her with a taxi driver but what the hell, she needed to talk to someone. The driver was an older gentleman. He had a round face. He may be a bit plump. Almost a Benny Hill look a like. Probably more of a gentleman though.

"How do you know I'm crying about a man?"

"Isn't it the only reason such a pretty young lady like yourself would be crying on her way to the airport in the middle of the night? There will be no flights for another few hours."

She found her conversation with this stranger to be soothing. He was after all someone to talk to. He would not judge her for being so irresponsible. To jet off with a man she barely knew. Love at first sight, no such thing. She continued her conversation.

"I have fallen for a man I thought I knew." She began to cry again, the tears ere much smaller this time.

"So you ran off to London with him did ya?"

She said nothing but looked at his gaze in the mirror.

"Then, ya get yourselves over here and find out ya didn't like him that much after all."

"He's married."

"That's what I said." He nodded his head but did not look in the mirror this time, "Ya didn't like him."

She smiled and looked out the window.

"That's right. I didn't like him."

"I've got a daughter about your age." Shelby saw the back of his head. White curls poked from beyond his black hat.

"And she has had the same problem?"

"Nope she got herself a real gent she did. I'm very thankful for that. She'd drive me and her mother right crazy if she didn't."

She smiled again.

"I did know a very lovely woman long ago. Her hair was red, red like a blazing fire. Her skin was so fair. And she had these tiny little freckles that sat carefully on her lovely pink cheeks. I remember her crying. Her heart was broken time and time again. She was about to give up on ever finding herself a husband." He waved left hand around. There was silence.

"Then what happened?" Shelby was curious.

"Oh she became very happy."

"Oh, and how was that?"

"She married me she did!"

After handing the therapeutic taxi driver one hundred American dollars for her ride to the airport; she leaned in and gave him a kiss on the cheek. He put his head down and blushed.

"Thank you miss." She stood on the curb as she watched the overstuffed taxi depart. Funny Shelby thought. She knew she would never see that man again. A shame, after touching her in a way that not even a mother could do. A total stranger. Mother's are biased.

For the next several hours Shelby would sit in front of the television that hung from the ceiling. It seemed to echo. Odd. A television echoing in an airport. It was so empty. So lonely. Tears trickled form her face, as she had to tell her friends and family what had happened on this trip. Not wanting to disappoint her mother, she would wait a few days before she would tell her family. She sat alone at the abandoned gate with wine still on her breath. She plucked a mint form her purse and unwrapped it.

"The only damn souvenir from London. A mint from Ophilia's and I'm going to eat it."

In a few hours or less, people would start to dwindle into the lonely airport and it would come to life. It would be morning and people will be buzzing around. Some leaving for a holiday as they call it over here, some lovers parting, some lovers having affairs just as she was certain someone may have thought the same of her. Some would be on business trips as Robert was supposed to be. Some people will say their good-byes and never see each other again. Sad she thought. She would sleep on the plane as she had not slept in nearly a day and a half.

I'll go home and take a bath and sleep. I'll sleep for a few days and then I will tell my mother. I won't be as upset if I wait. Shelby never liked for her family to worry about her. She would never call during a crisis until she had come up with the solution. Bring solutions, not the problem. Then they will never have to worry that way. She rested her head on her brown leather bag that sat on the seat next to her.

Mayla finished packing her suitcase for her trip to Tom's house.

"This is like a mini-vacation." She said to Vermin as she was digging through the refrigerator for food.

"Ya never know what's going to happen Vermin."

Despite the fact a hurricane is was heading directly for Florida as of this morning, Mayla and Tom planned to have fun with it. Stay up all night and watch movies, eat snacks, tell jokes and who know what else.

"Wouldn't it be a real shitter Vermin if a hurricane hit and my place went to hell in the middle of all my renovations? But then again if it did, the insurance company would have to pay for it. Might be cheaper that way."

Mayla turned to have one last look at her condo before she left hoping it would still be there when she returned.

"South Florida is expecting it's first hurricane of the year." Said a commentator on the television set, "The storm turned into hurricane Gunther on early Friday afternoon Florida time. Winds are topping eighty miles an hour and are expected to hit land within the next twenty- two to twenty-four hours. Your local news is next."

"Shit that's all I need." Shelby said. "I need to call Mayla again."

Shelby examined the handset to the payphone before she dialed not wanting gum stuck in her ear. It almost happened once before.

"Hi. This is Mayla, sorry I'm not home right now to take your call please leave a message and I'll get back to you." Beep.

"Mayla it's Shelby. Something terrible has happened. I need to talk to you. Please don't tell anyone about this call, not yet anyway. Especially in the office." She fought tears again. "I understand a hurricane is coming, that's the least of my worries. I'll try you when I get in."

Without leaving details Shelby hung up the phone. Looking around the terminal hoping Robert might pop up she saw only a few people begin to wonder in. No one resembled him. Not even close. Her flight would be leaving in another two hours.

"Up all night and half blitzed. Maybe I should have listened to him. I feel so dirty. Like a cheap prostitute. Wine and sex with a married man."

Slowly the skies began to lighten and more people were filling the empty terminal. Shelby would be boarding her plane in less than an hour. Still no sign of Robert.

"It's better this way. I have my respect and if what he said is true, than he can try to beg for my forgiveness after his home in Boca is done."

Mayla arrived at Tom's with her suitcase in one hand and Vermin in the other.

"What are you doing? Moving in?" Asked Tom as he opened the front door to greet her.

"You wish." Mayla smirked as she walked past him into his entryway. "Where's my bedroom?"

"Baby, I thought you were sleeping with me?"

"Funny Tom. Very funny. If you're looking for something to do, my car is filled with groceries and water. Help me please."

"Right away miss."

After filling the bathtubs and several empty buckets with water, Mayla helped Tom with the hurricane shutters. They were taking the hurricane very serious. After Hurricane Andrew in ninety-two they weren't about to take any chances. It was the most devastating natural disaster in Florida history. Thousands of people were left homeless and the Army was called in to assist in the clean up. There were speculations that more people died than originally reported. It was never broadcast because it was said that most of the deceased were migrant worker in the Florida City area and the government didn't want to cause uproar.

Tom turned on the television and put candles all around his home. He made certain he had plenty of C sized batteries for his portable radio.

"All set!" Tom said as he walked to the kitchen where Mayla was preparing a smoked salmon appetizer with onion and a dill sauce.

"Thought we may as well make the best of it." Mayla said as she put a cracker to Tom's mouth. "Eat."

"Not bad." Tom said with his mouth full.

"Got any movies?"

"Of course."

"Good evening." It was the local newscaster. "Hurricane Gunther's winds have recently reached wind gusts of up to ninety two miles per hour and the hurricane is heading west north west at thirteen miles per hour. All tolls have been lifted from the Florida Turnpike and the Sawgrass Expressway to make room for evacuations in all of South Florida. If you have not done so already, we are urging you to take precautions, fill your bathtubs with water. Make sure you have cash as the ATM machines will run out of cash after the hurricane if they are in working order. Be certain you have gas in your cars and your homes are boarded up. Now we have spoken with the hurricane center in regards to the question about taping your windows, their response? It will not help. Propane tanks should be filled." There was a pause as the newsman turned towards a woman handing him a paper; "We have just been informed the all flights in and out of Palm Beach, Dade and Broward Counties will be cancelled tonight at midnight."

"Well looks like we are in for a big one." Tom looked at Mayla as he stood with his hands on his hips, "But don't worry, I'll protect you. Did you bring your cell phone?"

"Yes it's charging in my room. Your room. My temporary room."

Michael finished moving all the lawn furniture inside his garage as Marlene came out to see how far he had gotten. He remembered the last year when he was all prepared for the hurricane that never hit. Not even a drop of rain. The entire house was camouflaged with its shutters. The streets were dead. People were hiding in their homes waiting for the "big one." It never came close.

"All done?"

"Yes." Michael replied wiping his forehead across his arm, "I can hardly believe there's a hurricane coming and there's not a cloud in the sky."

Marlene looked up as she put her hand over her eyes to shade the sun. "Your right. Not a cloud in the sky. Thank God for satellites and technology. Come in and get showered. You're stinky."

"I can't. I have to run out and get money and gas in the car. Did you put gas in yours?"

"Yes honey all gassed up."

Robert boarded the last flight possible into Miami from London. He had called his wife to assure her he would be there before the hurricane hit.

"Do you have the shutters on the house?"

"Yes. My brother helped to install them. Do you need me to pick you up from the airport?"

"No. I will take a taxi. I want you to finish getting ready for the hurricane. Make sure there is gas in the cars and."

"I have." Interrupted Neddie, "Just get here safely."

Robert paused to see if she would say anything about a strange phone call from an irate girl but the sound of her voice was pleasant as she was pleased to hear he was leaving London to come home and help with the storm and to be with his family.

"My flight is leaving shortly. I'll see you soon."

"Bye Robert." Neddie hung up the phone and tended to her business with their daughter.

The screeching sound of the tires made Shelby's eyes well up again. She thought the next time she landed in Miami she may have landed with a diamond on her finger. Or that at the very least, she would have landed with Robert.

"Jilted again." She whispered, "What is my problem? What did I do to deserve this?" Departing the plane was a very unpleasant task for her. To watch family and friends hugging and showing signs of emotion after being apart for weeks, months and years. There was no one to look after her. She thought she might have been feeling sorry for herself. Shelby departed from the plane and walked directly to the pay phones trying to reach Mayla again. Still no answer. Again she tried to phone her at work hoping by a fluke she would be there.

"Hi you have reached the desk of Mayla," Shelby felt the need to speak to Mayla's voice a mail in hopes it would relieve some of the pain she was feeling. She felt like she could explode.

"Mayla, I don't know who to call. I need to talk to you. I'm back in town and," she began to cry. "Robert is married. He told me after we, we." Trying to hold back the tears and not let anyone on the airport see her like this, "After he used me. I feel so badly. I threatened to call his wife. I'm so angry Mayla. I just don't know what to do. I don't know why this sort of thing happens to me all the time. I just. Oh never mind. I just wish you would call me. I'm in the Miami airport and I'll just take a taxi home."

Shelby hung up the phone and dried the tears from her face. After picking up her luggage she flagged down a taxi and went home where she would prepare for the hurricane by herself. Embarrassed by another broken heart, she wouldn't call anyone or tell anyone else what had happened. She could tell everyone her trip was cut short by the hurricane. That her and Robert both had to fly home to board up their houses. It was an excuse that would save her embarrassment. She began to feel better. And she knew her secret would be safe with Mayla and no one but Robert knew she was home.

After reaching her townhouse, Shelby turned on the television to monitor the status of the hurricane.

"Oh shit." She said as she stood in front of the TV eating a partially brown banana. "Gotta get to work. By myself."

Shelby wasn't as fortunate as the rest of the people in her firm with the electric hurricane shutters. She had to put on sheets of plywood that she had stored under the mattress in her spare bedroom. She thought it would be the perfect place to put the eye soars. After dragging them outside along with her electric drill her neighbor saw her struggle to put them up. The last time there was a hurricane coming; Jimmy from the mailroom helped her out.

"Hey Shelby need a hand?"

"Hi Tim. That would be great."

"Thought you were in London with that guy?"

"Had to cut it short." She replied as she handed Tim some screws. "We wanted to come back and board up the houses."

"Good thing you did. Looks like this one is coming right for us."

Tim was a young father with a beautiful wife. His sandy brown hair complimented his blue eyes. A native of Minnesota, the land of ten-thousand lake as he always called it, was always willing to help out his neighbors in a time of need.

"I saw that. I think it's a category five hurricane right now. Channel seven just said it was heading straight for South Miami and we should start to get the head of it this evening."

"Amazing isn't it? Look at the sky. Clear blue and the damn birds are flying around, I wonder if they know we have a hurricane coming?" His accent reminded her of a bouncing ball.

"Beats me."

"What are you going to do about the upstairs windows?" Tim asked.

"Nothing."

"Nothing? You have to do something."

"I won't be up there anyway. I may not stay here at all. I'm trying to reach a friend of mine."

"I see." Tim said oddly thinking to himself why she wouldn't be staying with the man that took her to London.

Tim read into Shelby's quiet demur. He was great at reading women as he is married to one for five years now. After drilling in the last screw Shelby asked if he would like anything to drink, iced tea? He declined as he had more work to do himself.

"If you need anything Shelby come on over and see us."

"Thanks Tim."

Shelby filled her bathtubs with water. She continued to prepare herself for the hurricane by gathering batteries and candles then putting them on the stand by the front door.

"Last time I looked in this mirror is when I was on my way to see that lying bastard." Shelby stood in front of the mirror and examined herself closely. She had an intent staring contest with herself as she ridiculed her hair, "too frizzy, too blond." She decided to change her hair closer to her natural color. Then onto her eyes. "Crows feet. I have crows feet." Looking for other imperfections she notice tiny wrinkles around her mouth. "No one will ever want to be with me. No one will ever want to marry me. I won't be a blushing bride. I'll be an old hag that will have to wear a purple wedding dress to hide her fat and distract her facial imperfections." Tugging on her eyes and lips Shelby's heart began to hurt again. Not motivated to save herself from the hurricane she sat on the sofa and began to cry. The television's sound was muted by her sadness.

"The hurricane has changed direction as they always do, and is now looking to head closer towards the North Miami Hollywood area. If you have not done so already, we are asking those of you who live east of US1 to please evacuate. The Red Cross has set up shelters at the following schools the are listed below. Please remember that your family pet is not allowed at these shelters. Also, women who are pregnant and are in their third tri-mester you are being told to check into the hospital as when the pressure drops you may begin to go into labor. If you do not do this no one will be able to aid you once the hurricane has hit land. There will be no 911 service. Once again the tolls have been lifted on all toll roads to help with the evacuation process. The airport will be closing at midnight tonight. We have just been informed that The National Hurricane center may also want to evacuate all persons living east of I-95."

All the local television stations in South Florida reflected the news only. Reporters were at South Beach interviewing tourist and locals on the street. Many of them thought this to be a reason to have a party. Some of the tourist were upset when they found out they had to stay in the shelters after planning their trip to Florida and getting a room on the beach.

Shelby stayed snuggled on her couch with the afghan her grand-mother had given her. It reminded her of when she was young. She would stay at her grandmothers as a child when she was sick and could not go to school. Since her mother and father both worked, her mom would drop her off at her grandmothers. Her grandmother would spoil her with hot lemon and honeys.

"What are ya doing?" Tom asked as Mayla dialed her house to check her messages, "You didn't ask if you could use my phone."

"May I use your phone?" Mayla turned to look at Tom.

"No."

"Funny."

Mayla continued to dial her house and punch in her code to receive her messages. Her time with Tom has been fun so far. She hadn't felt uncomfortable in the least bit.

"Something's wrong with Shelby." Mayla said as she hung up the phone. "She seemed pretty distraught. She flew home Tom."

"Really? Well maybe you should try and call her."

"I will."

"Honey, I'm heading out." Michael called to Marlene who stood in the kitchen organizing the canned food. "I'm going to go see if I can get some cash from any of the ATM machines."

"Okay," Marlene answered back, "Bring your cell phone!"

"Got it."

It was beginning to fall to dusk as Michael backed out of his drive-way. The sky had a funny color to it. Orangish. The winds were picking up ever so slightly. Mother Nature was now beginning to show her signs of hurricane Gunther. After putting the car in drive, Michael's cell phone rang. It was Max.

"Hello?" Michael answered.

"Michael I just spoke to Marlene. She said I could reach you on your cell phone. She is such a lovely woman. You are a very lucky man Michael."

"Yes I am." He replied.

"I could hear your children in the background. It sounds like you run a very happy content home. It's such a shame that not everyone can have such a life. Wouldn't it be horrible if that were taken away from you? By the way, did you find the envelope Michael?"

Michael did not answer. He just held the phone to his ear and let Max continue, "Michael, do we have a bad reception? Michael are you there?"

Michael's blood began to boil as Max spoke to him in such a degrading manner.

"Michael, I know you are there. Why can't you answer me? Have you not learned anything? Didn't the break into the office scare you enough? Or how about Mrs. Riley's Brother? Mr. Riley will never stray again. He will never tell myself or Philppo he wants out again."

"You keep my family out of this you son of a bitch." He was yelling into his cell phone.

"Michael, Michael, Michael. You knew what you were getting into. You should hire such incompetent people to work for you."

There was a click on the other end. A click that sent chills through his spine. A click that echoed over and over again his head. A click that was the final straw.

Michael's anger overtook him as he began to swerve in and out of traffic.

"That bastard." Making an aggressive U-turn in the middle of the road he found himself on his way to Shelby's house.

"I'll get your fucking envelope."

Michael could only think of his wife and daughters as he drove to Shelby's house.

"Not my family." He began to lose his composure as he thought of what Max had done to the Riley family.

Shelby had fallen asleep on the sofa. When she woke up she went upstairs taking a bottle of Opus that she had been saving for a special occasion. She studied the bottle running her fingers along the curvaceous edges. Holding the bottle to the light to see if there had been any sediment sleeping at the bottom. She read the label over and over again. Opus, Opus, Opus, it rang in her mind. Ninety-seven. Not a bad year for Opus One. Robert Mondovi, Robert Mondavi, Opus One, Nineteen ninety-seven. Uncorking the bottle had been a task that she had enjoyed. A master at it, so she thought. She twirled the cork under her nose knowing that a wine master knows there is no logical reason for doing this. She poured herself a tiny bit in a Rydel glass swirled it, sniffed it, held it to the light, then tossed her head back and poured the wine in. She would let it sit for a moment on her tongue, as it would slowly creep down her throat.

"Lovely." She poured herself another glass this time filling it half way. "You breath." She pointed and spoke to the glass.

Shelby learned about wine from her father. As a child, he would teach about the different types of grapes and the different regions they had come from. Mr. Peterson would allow her to have wine at the dinner table during the holidays even though she was under age. He wanted to educate her. Teach her. Mrs. Peterson however was not too fond of the idea. During the summer months, Mr. Peterson used to make strawberry and dandelion wine. Shelby used to sip it from the wooden spoons that her father used. Since she was three, she had always thought that a wooden spoon was used for making wine.

"What the hell." She said as she lit some candles.

After putting a CD in her small stereo in her bathroom, she flipped the switch for the whirlpool as her naked silhouette reflected on the uncovered window behind her. Sinking into the hot bubbling bathtub with her favorite wine in her hand.

"Bastard."

She was taken away by the humming sound that came from around her.

"Taxi!" Robert yelled as he waved his arm in the air. He looked desperate to get out of the heat. It was hot and muggy. The taxi driver noticed Robert was perspiring under his nose.

"Everything alright mon?" The taxi driver was obviously from Jamaica.

"Fine. No it's not fine. I am so afraid I have really messed things up."

"Where would you like to go mon?"

"I want you to take me to Coconut Creek."

"No problem. I take you there and everything will be all right. So you mess things up with your woman?"

"Am I that obvious?"

"I can tell by your face. My father has that look when he upset my mother. She makes him crazy. Just crazy."

The taxi driver pulled away from the curb. "I tell you mon, you get a woman you love, you never let her go." He looked in his rearview mirror as he tossed his dread locks to one side of his head, "Woman. Woman they be funny. They don't forgive so easy. So that is why it be best not to mess things in the first place."

"I'll remember that next time."

Mayla hung up the phone and turned to Tom with a puzzled look on her face.

"No answer."

"Did you try her on her cell phone?"

"Yes but there was no answer."

Shelby could not hear her phones ring. The smooth sound of jazz and the buzzing of the bath overtook the ringing of the phones. Her eyes were closed as she relaxed. The wine was working well as a sedative. An occasional branch from the ficus tree would brush up the against the window. It was the only other sound she could hear.

"Did you leave her a message and tell her you could be reached here?"

"I did."

"Then she'll call. Don't worry. You hungry?"

"Yes actually I am."

"Then make us something to eat." Tom smiled.

"You'll have bugs and lizards if you talk to me like that again."

"Hurry up. I'm hungry. Pour me a glass of wine while you're at it."

"I saw some in your garage."

"Saw what?" asked Tom.

"Bugs. You will have bugs."

The night had closed in and most people were glued to their television set to monitor the status of the hurricane.

"We are standing out here on the beach in Ft. Lauderdale and if you look behind me you will notice the waves are getting to be quite high. We have surfers in the water taking advantage of the waves. We are not so sure this is a good idea due to under currents."

"What a bunch of dorks." Mayla mumbled as she shook her head.

"Who? The surfers or the news caster?"

"Both. I wouldn't be out there, then the reporters are so dramatic."

"It's all about ratings my dear Mayla."

"Got any movies?"

"What kind baby?"

"R rated is as crazy as I get."

The man standing on the beach continued filling the airwaves with his repetitive report as Tom searched through his armoire for a movie.

"The winds here are growing fierce. The hurricane has made a definite turn towards the north. It is due to reach landfall around 3 a.m. The Broward County Sheriffs office is making sure everyone has evacuated east of I-95. This hurricane is to be taken very seriously."

"I'm going to try calling Shelby again." Mayla stood up and went to Tom's telephone in the kitchen. Tom sat on the sofa and watched her dial. He studied her once again.

I wonder what she would be like, how would it be to have her? Is she the faithful type? Of course she is. She doesn't date just anyone. She obviously cares for her friends and family. What religion is she anyway? Nice shape. Not too thin. I don't like thin women. They may break during childbirth. She can cook. She's smart, she works for me. I wonder how her mouth tastes. Maybe one day I will find out.

"Shelby? It's me Mayla, pick up the phone. I'm worried about you. I don't know where you are. I'm at Tom's and we're about to watch a movie. Please call me at his house or on my cell as soon as you get this message."

"Still no answer?" Tom asked.

"No."

"Do you think we should drive to her house and see if she's home?"

"She may have gone to her mothers or some other friends house. What is she so upset about?"

"I'm not sure. I think she may have had an argument with Robert."

"We can take a ride. But we need to make it quick, it's getting pretty windy out there."

"I'm sure you're right. She may have gone to her mothers."

"So you want to stay here and just snuggle with me?" Tom moved in on Mayla.

She pushed him away, "Get away from me pal. You wouldn't know what to do with me after you had me."

Tom pouted off to the television where he put in an old videotape of The Wizard of Oz.

"How appropriate." Mayla said as she sipped her wine and sat on Tom's brown leather sofa with her legs tucked under her.

"Hey honey." Michael was out of breath as he walked through the door that led to the garage. "I'm sorry it took me so long but I had a hard time finding any ATM's with any cash left in them."

"I was beginning to get worried. The girls are in the playroom. I'm going to put them to bed here in a minute."

Michael moved close to Marlene, "So will you be able to give me your undivided attention?"

"Absolutely. I'll put them to bed now."

Marlene put the girls to bed and read them a bedtime story from a book of fairy tales.

Michael stood in the kitchen and made a phone call to Max on his cell phone.

"Everything has been taken care of."

"Did you get the envelope?"

"Like I said, everything has been taken care of. You're an intelligent man Max. Figure it out."

Michael hung up on Max to give him a taste of his own medicine. He was feeling very powerful at the moment.

"Bastard."

"What did you say honey?"

It was Marlene standing in the doorway to the kitchen.

"Oh nothing. I was just thinking about this damn storm. I hope we'll be okay."

"I'm sure we will come out just fine."

The taxi driver brought Robert to Coconut Creek like he had asked. They were only there for a few moments before he was taken to his final destination in North Miami. The Jamaican taxi driver sped off leaving Robert standing in his driveway at his home. His house was covered in hurricane shutters. He could see a tiny bit of light peeking through them as he walked to the front door.

"Hi Bob." It was Neddie. His wife. "We need to hurry. I'm glad you flew home for this but we need to leave right away. I thought we could drive to our home in Bonita Springs but we will not make it. We'll have to go to my sister's house instead. I hope you don't mind but I've packed a bag for you. I thought we could get out of here quicker." She was scattering around as she spoke to him.

"I don't mind." Robert said as he looked for his daughter.

"She is at my sisters. I brought her there this afternoon. I thought I would wait for you. Are you all right? Is something wrong with you? You're sluggish."

"I'm fine." He wasn't convincing.

Robert walked through all the rooms in his house carefully studying each one in case the hurricane decided to take his home away from him.

"Did you fill the cars with gas?"

"Yes of course I did."

"Did you?"

Neddie interrupted, "What do you think? Of course I did. Now let's go." He never seemed to trust her enough to handle an emergency.

Robert checked on his Ferrari that sat in the garage covered with a tarp to protect it from any falling debris. He sighed as he stood watching it as if it were supposed to talk to him.

"Hello Bob. The car began to speak. *We have known each other for what? Six months now? I can tell by the expression on your face that you are not as cool as you usually are. I guess you missed me. So what's happened? Blow it with that girl? How would I know? I am a woman to, after all you named me,*" She began to sing "*My name is Lola, I am a show car.*" Then she spoke again; "*If I were a man I may not be scolding you. I'd be telling you; way to go Bob! But I think we can have this conversation. Fess up, you messed things up with that girl didn't you? And your wife? She knows nothing about the affair you are having with this girl does she? Oh yes, I know you are leaving.* His very own car was being sarcastic. The car he loved and cherished so much was giving him a hard time.

"Shut up Lola." He closed the garage door behind him.

CHAPTER THIRTEEN

Most of South Florida has now settled into their homes to brace themselves for the largest hurricane since Andrew in ninety-two. The storm is continuing to intensify as it was due to hit land early Saturday morning. Winds were topping eighty-five miles per hour. The beaches from Miami to West Palm Beach became deserted except for a few patrol cars and news trucks with satellite dishes driving up and down the coast on A1A. The usually crowed beaches that normally held thousands of out of town visitors had now become a sleepy ghost town.

"I am so tired." Mayla yawned as the credits to the movie ran past the television set.

"Would you like me to tuck you in?" asked Tom.

"I think I can manage." Mayla stood and walked towards the window where she would pause for a brief moment. It was past midnight and the winds were beginning to toss the branches from the palm trees back and forth. The rain danced on the streets.

"Looks like we have the beginning of our storm." Tom said as he stood next to Mayla. "Seriously Mayla," He placed his arm on her shoulder, "If this storm frightens you, you can sleep in my room; Naked!"

Mayla didn't smile as she turned and replied graciously, "Okay."

Tom was left standing there in his bare feet on the cold tile floor. "Was she serious?" He thought to himself experiencing the same awkward moment he had at work the other day. He stood watching her gracefully slow walk towards the room that he had assigned to her. "Maybe she will get lost. No don't go that way; turn back, to the left! Come back!" Tom talked to himself hoping she would get lost and end up in his room.

"I love you." Marlene said as she lay on top of Michael stroking his hair. "I should get the girls and bring them in the room now." Kissing his chin then pressing her hands against his chest to lift her off the bed, "Miss me while I'm gone."

"Don't leave. Not yet." Michael tugged on her arm and pulled her close to his chest again. "Please just lay here for a while longer. I want to feel your breath on my neck. I want to feel you again."

"I may fall asleep if you do that to me again."

"Then that means I have done my job as a man." Michael smirked as he struck a masculine pose for Marlene.

"You'll never have to prove to me that you're a man."

Her naked body was glowing by candlelight as she moved her lips towards Michael's ear. "You are such a demanding man. Why do I stay with you?"

"For that reason. Because I am so demanding." Michael smiled as he flipped his wife over and rolled on top of her. "I'm going to have you again."

"Can you hear that?"

"What? The only thing I want to hear is you."

"The wind. It's very angry."

"Make love to me again honey. Just one more time. For the sake of the hurricane."

The howling sound of the wind defied the music they were making.

"Mayla. Mayla." Tom was frantically shaking her to wake up.

"Hmmm." She rolled over, "What is it?"

"Get up! You have to see this!"

"What is it?" While trying to wake herself up, she rubbed her eyes.

"These winds are unbelievable! There's some tree already down! This wasn't supposed to hit until late morning! It's only six in the morning."

"Why are you getting me up?" She was groggy.

"You have to see this!"

Tom began to pull on Mayla as if he were a child on Christmas morning.

"I'm up. I'm up."

"Come see this!" Tom walked Mayla into his living room to the front door where only a small window remained uncovered. "Look."

"Oh my god." Mayla began to wake up as she saw several large branches lining the road. The neighbor across the street had lost a Banyan tree. It looks as if it landed on top of their house.

"Maybe we should turn on the television." Mayla said as she began to walk towards the set.

"No power."

"No power?" She asked.

"It's already out."

"We've lost power already?"

"I have the radio. We can listen to it. Do you want to stay up?"

"Ya, sure." She said softly.

"Want to drink something?"

"Coffee."

"No power." Tom reminded her.

"How did they do it?"

"How could people have ever lived without electricity?"

Tom shrugged. "So what'll ya have?"

"I'll have some cranberry juice."

"Sounds good."

Mayla and Tom remained huddle on the sofa in the living room listening to the small portable radio. She lay close to him leaning on his arm, as she was still sleepy.

The beginning of the storm had swooped into South Florida greeting them with winds of thirty miles an hour, then forty, even up to sixty miles an hour in some areas. Trees were being tossed around along with lawn furniture and plastic garbage cans. The rain could barely touch the ground, as the fierce winds would not allow it.

"Michael," Marlene woke Michael. "We fell asleep! We need to get the girls and go downstairs. It's getting pretty bad outside." Marlene seemed to be panicking.

Michael sat up immediately as he heard the howling wind and the rain pounding on the roof.

"Oh jeez." He flipped the covers off him and jogged towards the girl's room. "Come on girls! Time to get up."

"It's not time to get up daddy." Samantha stayed snuggled in her bed.

"Yes honey it is." He took the blankets off the sleeping angle and carried her downstairs. Tallie followed behind.

Marlene scurried to gather pillows and blankets from the linen closet in the hallway to put in the powder room downstairs.

"Good morning girls." Marlene bent to kiss Tallie and Samantha.

"Mommy I'm tired." Tallie's light blue eyes and blond curly hair caught her mother's heart.

"I know sweetie, but we have to sleep downstairs right now."

Michael took the pillows of the sofa and lined the closet floor with them. He brought the radio, water and flashlights setting them on the floor in the corner.

Marlene looked at Michael as Tallie wrapped her arms around her mother's leg.

"Come on girls this will be like we're camping out! It will be fun! Look here, we have flashlights and water! What else would you like to bring?"

"Daddy I would like to bring marshmallows! We can make smores."

"I don't think we can have a cookout in this closet but we can get you some marshmallows. As a matter of fact why don't you girls get a few things you would like to bring to our camp site."

"I can't believe how this storm snuck up on us. I thought they said it was going to hit mid-morning. We need to turn on the television to find out where it is."

The hurricane managed to spare the electricity in the Weston area. However it wouldn't be long before the storm will rip through the neighborhood knocking over any trees or power lines that dare stand in it's way.

Michael turned on the television as Marlene sat down on the sofa in front of it. Fear was beginning to overtake her body as she sat biting her nails.

"If you look here," said the weatherman; "We have several serious storm cells moving through the area. What you may be experiencing is not the actual hurricane, but the storms surrounding the eye. It will continue to worsen throughout the morning. The rain has already reached up to seven inches in the Southwest Broward County area. We are live now to our news crew who are in the downtown Hollywood area."

"Richard we are here in the downtown Hollywood area and if you will notice I am standing in two feet of water this is what used to be East Hollywood Boulevard. The rain has taken over the roadway. We are asking that everyone please stay inside. Children should not be allowed to play in this water as it maybe contaminated and also because there maybe down power lines, and if there are, they may be electrocuted."

Channel Seven rambled on as Marlene looked over to Michael. She watched him as he studied the television. She felt safe with him. He would protect her and the girls from the monster that was slowly creeping across South Florida. She felt sinfully happy. I'm so lucky she thought. What a wonderful man. He's an incredible father. He's intelligent. He buys me flowers. He holds me at night. He would never have to tell me he loves me, I feel it.

Marlene rubbed his shoulder then kissed his ear; "I'm going to check on the girls."

"Mayla we need to get in the bathroom." Tom was dragging a twin-sized mattress off the bed Mayla had slept on that night. "I guess I'll get you in bed one way or another just make sure you wear that sexy little number I told you to pack."

"Funny I guess I forgot to pack it. It's a shame. It had crotchless panties. I guess I'll just have to get the candles and flashlights instead."

"You better grab Vermin."

Tom was bent over securing the mattress on the floor of the bathroom.

"Here we are." Mayla balanced the box of candles on her hip as she handed Vermin to him.

"We'll hang you from the shower curtain rail." Tom spoke to Vermin as he hung him.

"Do you think we need anything else?"

"I don't think much else will fit."

Mayla and Tom sat next to the bathtub as the winds began to pick up speed. The night sky never had a chance to greet the morning sun as the storm robbed them of their usual daily ritual. It was still dark as the rains continued to fall. By now you could hear debris banging against the stucco on the house.

"Great." Tom said. "I just painted the outside of this house in April."

Mayla listened to Tom, as she thought about her own home. She couldn't imagine ever losing it to a storm. After all it was her grandma Pearl's home. As a child Mayla would visit her after school and her grandmother would take her for walks on the beach collecting broken shells. Sometimes they would make necklaces and bracelets from the tide beaten seashells. Afterwards her grandmother would take her for an ice cream at Etta's Ice Cream Parlor. Mayla would always order a banana split with chocolate, strawberry and caramel, just a few nuts.

"Aren't you going to have one grandma?" Mayla as a child would ask.

"Oh no sweetheart, not today." Knowing Mayla could never finish her banana split, Grandma Pearl would wait until Mayla ate what she could and then Grandma Pearl would finish it for her.

"Just a taste sunshine. That's all I need. I need to make sure they are giving you their finest ice cream."

Grandma loved ice cream just as much as Mayla. Etta's ice cream parlor is gone now. A man from South America had come and bought it back in the mid-nineties. If grandma knew, it would break her heart. The South American man had changed it into a beauty supply store. Mayla would frequent the store and pretend she was interested in the shampoos and brushes where in fact the only reason she had gone there was to picture where her and her grandmother used to sit and share the ice cream. It was in the corner against the front window where pony tail holders and hairpieces now rest that Mayla had told her grandmother of her first boyfriend. She was ten. It was in the same booth that grandma had told Mayla about how her father had proposed to her mother. It was there that Mayla would inform her grandmother Pearl about the business she was going to start by selling the jewelry that her and her grandmother had made from the shells. Her first customers would be her classmates. She only sold a few. They were too pretty and all became her favorite. She couldn't sell them. Her business didn't last long.

When her grandmother passed away and Mayla and her mother were sorting through her things, they ran across several bracelets and necklaces each in their own box. Mayla began to cry when she opened the first box, and cry harder when she opened the second and third. She had lost the ones she had made when she was a little girl. That evening before sundown Mayla went to visit her grandmother's grave by herself. She thanked her for holding her little treasures for so many years. Before leaving Mayla carefully placed a necklace on her grandmother's head stone. Now she holds the ones that her grandmother had for so long, close to her heart. Mayla hopes that someday she can share the same stories with her children and grandchildren. Sweet memories.

"I wonder how my condo is doing? I hope it's all right. I just spent a fortune on renovations. Hey Tom, is my cell phone in that box?"

Tom sifted through the box lifting out her cell phone and holding it up, "Here you are."

"Just in case someone worries about me."

"You have one less person who worries about you."

"What do you mean?" Mayla's face was covered by her hair as she checked the battery supply on her phone.

"There is one less person that knows you will be okay."

"Really." She smiled and looked up, "How is that?"

"That one less person is with you." Tom's response was serious as there was no crack in his voice and his eyes held her stare. Mayla felt uncomfortable, as she never thought she would be put in this position while preparing for a hurricane. *Does he plan to kiss me? What do I do now? What do I say? Now how am I supposed to respond to such a remark? My body gesture must be that of a clown. I'm certain I look silly.* Then without even thinking she blurted out as she held up her phone, "Let's call my Mom. She will be happy I am being taken care of. That I am safe." Stupid she thought. *What a dumb thing to say. Normally I am so confident. Why am I like jelly? My toes are numbing and I am certain my face looks like a tomato.* To embarrassed to confront his eyes she scrambled through the box for a flashlight.

"We have two flashlights. We can have a flashlight war!"

Tom sat back against the ivory walls and said nothing as he watched her playfully try to work her way out of his words.

"Save the flashlights. We may need them. But we can turn on the radio, let's see if we can find us some romantic music, or maybe some old Marvin Gaye."

"Thank God he's back." Mayla thought to herself. "But there's no room for us to dance baby." She continued to pick through the box, "You brought your video camera?"

"Thought you may want to make a movie with me." Tom smirked.

"Maybe someday." She smiled and leaned back up against the wall with him. "Listen to that wind! I've never heard anything like it! Should we have another peek outside?" She sounded curious.

"Let's go see." Tom stood and stretched his arm out to Mayla to help her up, "Can't be any harm in it."

They peered through the small window like starving little children in a candy shop window.

"Unbelievable." Remarked Tom. "My neighbors barrel tile roof is beginning to come off! Look at that tree! I need to gather a few more things. I really don't like the looks of this."

"Oh my." Mayla stretched to stand on the top of her toes as she took her turn looking out the window. The sky had turned a dark green and the wind was picking up speed. There were branches, garbage cans, toys and some lawn furniture blowing through the streets with the rain, "Come on Mayla," Tom pulled her away from the window, "Get in the bathroom and listen to the radio. I will be right there."

Tom returned with another cardboard box and a large cooler. "Just in case. These things scare me. I'll never forget those victims of hurricane Andrew. I don't want to be one of them."

Mayla began to grow a little nervous as she felt Tom's sense of insecurity. "I'm sure we'll be alright." She said as she took the box from him.

Tom gave Mayla a sweet smile, "I know we will. I just had to get a few things that can never be replaced."

"Like what?" She asked as she sat on the cooler.

"Pictures. Tokens of my past. That sort of thing."

"I see. May I have a look?" Mayla lit a candle to brighten the room.

"Sure. This is my family." He held the picture out to Mayla and sat on the toilet, "My Mom and Dad, my little sister Melanie and my older brother Mark. It's an old picture."

"I can see that. Look at you! That has to be the ugliest sweater I have ever seen."

"That was in eighty-four. It was the last picture we had taken together before my brother was killed in a car accident."

"Oh." Mayla's eyes grew wide, "I'm sorry."

"It was a long time ago. I miss him." He stared at the picture studying it for a while; Mayla said nothing as she watched him. "I wanted to be just like him. He was my hero. Except he wanted to be a doctor. He never made it through his first years of med school. It was a bad night. Storming pretty hard and he couldn't see the road. A car was coming from the other direction and I guess they didn't know who was in whose lane, besides we really didn't want to know. We were satisfied no one was drinking. He and two other people died."

"That's terrible. I'm so sorry."

"I'm okay talking about it. It happened such a long time ago."

He put the picture back in the box face up. "You just always have to remember how short life is. Try not to hold grudges. Try something new every chance you get. Treat people like you want to be treated. Life is simple yet so complex."

"I hear ya. I had no idea you had this side to you Tom. I just always thought you were a bit of an egotistical male, well, pig."

Tom's face was left expressionless as Mayla voiced her opinion of him. There was no smile, no sinister remarks. Just a blank stare that left her speechless.

"Like I said, get what you can when you can. Life is short." Tom reached for Mayla's hand and held it tightly. She thought this might be the moment he would lean in to kiss her. Her heart tingled and stomach knotted up. She couldn't look him directly in his eyes in fear of rejection.

What if he didn't kiss her? He just told her "life is short" why wouldn't he kiss her? Maybe he was more of a gentleman than she realized.

"We should go have some fun. Maybe next weekend. If there's anything left of the keys after this hurricane, come diving with me."

He spoke to her like he was her brother. After that she wasn't afraid to look at him. Shocked, relieved and even somewhat disappointed she said, "K."

CHAPTER FOURTEEN

The wind was twirling throughout South Florida throwing innocent trees to the ground leaving the roots exposed to the drowning rain. Unprotected windows were blown out. Cars were being turned over on their sides. Awnings were blown off of the businesses in the downtown are of Hollywood. The streets were flooded hiding sidewalks leaving it up to traffic lights and stop signs to determine where the road used to be. Slowly the hurricane moved into South Florida destroying homes and even mercilessly taking some lives. Families huddled together in the bathrooms and closets while their homes shook around them. Other people remained in shelters at local schools having to leave their family pets behind. Fear would reap through South Florida as the hurricane spun through. There were only a few select areas out west that remained with electrical power.

Tears ran down Marlene's face as she sat rocking on the closet floor with Tallie in her lap. Michael sat embracing the other child with his left hand and rubbed his wife's back with the other.

"We'll be alright honey." Trying to comfort Marlene, Michael then suggested they play a game.

"What game Daddy?" Samantha turned to look at her father. "We can't go outside."

"I know baby. We can play I went to my grandmothers house."

Michael had such a way of soothing Marlene in tough times. Like the day of their wedding. Guests were beginning to pour into the hotel on the beach where they had their reception. An elder female guest that had been admiring the cake accidentally dropped her punch on the wooden floor next to the table. She left to retrieve napkins to clean up the spill but before she could return, the best man slipped on the juice and tried to balance himself by grasping the table. Unfortunately he still lost his balance as the table tipped over on top of him and he fell to the floor. He lay on his back in his black tuxedo as other guests rushed to his side to see if he were hurt. Thankfully he was not, but the cake was destroyed as it sat on top of his tuxedo. There was one tier which Michael and his best man had managed to salvage for the cutting of the cake. They looked like little boys in a sandbox. Building a castle as they occasionally licked their fingers.

"Look honey!" He smiled at her proudly. "It's beautiful!" Michael's best man stood in the background with frosting all over him. His look was of pure guilt. He felt responsible. Marlene began to laugh at the pitiful sight. She liked Joe. It wasn't his fault.

"That'll teach you Joe!" She waved her finger as she scolded him, "No picking at the frosting!"

After reminiscing of their wedding she knew she would be just fine. The storm will clear up and then they would have to clean up the mess outside their home.

Michael stood to open the door from time to time to check on the house. The shutters seem to be doing their job as the house remained in tact.

"I think I'm going to have a walk around the house." He stood as he sat Samantha on the floor next to her mother. "I'll be right back."

He walked through the entire house looking in the kitchen, the bedrooms and even in the garage where there was a little flooding. It seems the storm so far had spared them much of the anguish that the rest of

South Florida will endure. The winds were still blowing and the rain was still coming down as Michael returned to his family.

"We'll be fine. Remind me to write a letter to the company that we bought those hurricane shutters from. They seem to be holding up just fine. Now, lets play that game we talked about."

He came through again. His wife watched him play with the girls. Peace filled her soul as the deadly hurricane whirled around outside their home. It was if there were a shield not allowing it to touch the family. Marlene began to play the game with the girls and her husband.

Robert remained with his wife Neddie at her sister's house in the Weston area. They never took cover in the bathroom or closet. Yet they remained in the family room with the radio blasting the news as her sister served mimosas.

"Have to make the best of it! To hurricane Gunther!" Selma said as she handed them the orange juice concoction. She is a petite little blond with green eyes who is very close to sister. She knew of the tough times Robert and Neddie were having. Hoping they would work it out as she liked Robert and didn't want to see their daughter having to run between homes as her and Neddie had to do when they were young. It would be tough life for her.

Not wanting to bring up the home in Boca or what was happening to the couple Selma remained in high spirits. In return, it seemed to relieve some of the stress Robert and Neddie were feeling on their upcoming divorce. Some temporary relief. Almost like an antacid. The hurricane and mimosas. Perfect combination for happiness.

"Would anyone care for a breakfast bar? Or I could get crazy and make some lox with onions and capers."

Robert drifted when Selma spoke of lox. The last time he had salmon it was with the keeper of the heart that he had broken. He remained silent as he heard Selma and Neddie gabbing in the background. It's over now.

Neddie was beginning to question weather or not Robert was having an affair. She felt what happens, happens. They had tried for a very long time to try and make their relationship work by going to a marriage counselor several times a month. But the birth of their daughter, no matter how wonderful of a gift from God she had been, they no longer had the time for each other as they once did. Traveling to Europe thrice yearly for two to three weeks at a time, and taking several golfing weekends in between to break up the long wait before the next trip.

She did not want a divorce. She wanted it work but had come to realize that saving her marriage was not the most important and only thing in her life. She began to lose touch with herself. Her self-esteem began to drop, as she had not worked in several years so she could accommodate Robert on business trips. He did not like to travel alone. She quite doing the things she used to do. Working out. Cooking classes. Biking daily to the beach, golfing with her girlfriends. She fell into a depression where 'he' was the only thing that had mattered to her anymore. The harder she tried the more he pulled away. She let him be. She knew she could no longer make him happy. It was time for her now. She is a civil woman and does not want her daughter to see "mommy and daddy" fighting. She wants her to understand that mommy and daddy love her very much. Not having a Ward and June Cleaver type of childhood herself, she wanted to make it different for her child.

Neddie finally came to her senses when she saw a woman on a rampage in the Aventura mall screaming at her husband as he sat in the crowded food court holding hands with a girl who had to be half his age. The scorned woman had a young boy about seven years old standing next to her holding her hand. He had to be their son. He put his head down into his hand and began to tear as his mother was screaming and crying at her husband. People would turn and stare at the woman when they passed by. They thought she was crazy. The young girl quickly retrieved her hand from the married man.

Neddie understood her pain as she sometimes felt like screaming at Robert. But it was the boy she could not come to terms with. He stood helpless while his mother was suffering with the embarrassing pain of finding her husband with someone else. Neddie wanted to comfort the boy. It was then, at that moment that she had realized that her and Robert had grown apart. It would be best to set him free then to ever have to endure the pain that that woman had felt. That evening she told Robert how much she loved him and wanted to remain civil, but she wanted a divorce. She told him she wanted the home they live in now and that he would have to find another place to live and she would allow him to stay until he did. However, if he had an affair with anyone while still living under the same roof he would have to leave immediately. He agreed it was time for them to separate. Since the agreement they became more tolerable of each other. They would still continue to play golf once or twice a week at the club that they belonged to and on occasion make love here and there as they still had an attraction for each other. But it soon fizzled when Neddie thought it would be too hard for him to leave if they continued. He obliged and had not made love to her in months. They sleep in separate rooms.

CHAPTER FIFTEEN

The lower level of the townhouse remained quiet. Tree branches banged up against the townhouse's outer salmon colored walls. The windows upstairs in all the rooms look as if they had been blasted out. Rain was blowing in and only one panel of the white sheer curtain that was hung on an iron bar above the bathtub remained flying and twirling through the air. Shelby had lied peacefully in her bath with remnants of glass from the window, which had cut her several times. Surrounding her was an empty bottle of Opus and her wineglass. It remained in tact yet sadly slumped on it side. A dabble of wine left in its chamber. With the cold water running, her eyes were closed. Her lips had turned blue and her damp blond hair hung on her naked shoulders. She was breathless, colorless and limp, as she was dead.

The winding stream of water left the bathroom and eventually would make a boy scouts trail to her room circling around her bed and then down the stairs before she would be found. Wet pictures of her family lie on the floor. Pictures from the last trip her family had together visiting the Grand Canyon. They stood happily smiling with the orange and red stones behind them. "Cheese" for the camera. There was a picture of her best friend Amy from high school. They stood in their caps and gowns from their high school graduation. Their arms were around each other, "cheese" For the camera. A photo of her mother and father celebrating their twenty-fifth wedding anniversary lied on its back. "Cheese" for the camera.

The flower duvet dripping. The closet doors were open with clothes scattered about from the gusts of wind that made their way though her bedroom.

The helpless girl lay peacefully in her bathtub in her home. Died alone, died with a broken heart.

The mirror on the lower level of the townhouse that hung by the front door would be sad. This mirror that had seen her through many dates, the mirror that helped her with her lipstick and hair would remain lonely, never to see the face of Shelby again.

Chapter Sixteen

The clouds rolled out of South Florida. Slowly curious people would emerge from their homes to inspect the damage done to their houses and their neighborhood.

A trailer park off I-595 had been destroyed leaving pieces of aluminum in surround the poles and trees that managed to survive. It looks as if high school kids ran crazy in a yard toilet papering the trees. Dogs wondered the streets looking for where their homes used to be as pets were not allowed in the shelters.

Florida Power and Light had a convoy of trucks pacing up and down I-95 and I-595. Soon much of the power would be restored to most of the community. Some neighborhoods however were not so lucky. They would have to wait for days for power to be returned to them.

The airport would reopen. Public transportation resumed. As the community would try to return to it's usual schedule. Some families would have to find a new place to live. The American Red Cross was called in to feed those who had lost their home. The more fortunate people who lost nothing would volunteer their time and help with clean up.

Unfortunately, in the downtown area of Ft. Lauderdale looters would start moving in and jumping through storefront windows and taking what ever they could carry. Televisions, clothing, food from restaurant freezers, narcotics from the drug store such as morphine, Demerol, or any drug that have some sort of street value. It will be chaos for a few hours before the Sheriffs office moves in to take control.

News crews stilled roamed the streets looking for anything to keep them on the air a few hours longer. To make them the number one station in South Florida.

Tom and Mayla felt relief as they emerged from the tiny bathroom. Tom suffered no damage to the inside of his home. He went outside to inspect his house. He lost his favorite orange tree and a garbage can that he had forgotten to bring into the garage. A few tiles on the roof had been blown off. There was only minor damage and he was satisfied.

They would spend the next few minutes calling their family to inform them that they had weathered hurricane Gunther.

"Looks like I made it through the storm! I only lost a garbage can and unfortunately my favorite orange tree." Tom seemed pleased as he opened and closed doors throughout his home. Mayla followed close behind. "Will you come with me to my house?" She asked with innocently. "I may need to stay a few days if anything has happened to my house, or if not, I'm sure that Shelby wouldn't mind if I."

"Not a problem. Baby. You can stay here, and on the way back from your house we can stop by to check on Shelby." He smiled, "Lets go."

Tom's electrical power was restored within a matter of hours.

Mayla left Vermin behind as she went to check on her home. It had only been a few hours since the departure of the hurricane. As she opened the door to her condo she thought she would find her new granite counter tops crumbled on the floor. The paint peeled off the walls and her new drapes for certain would be out to sea. She found no damage to her condo. Only the landscaping had been destroyed and a few units had lost some windows as they were snowbirds and did not cover them before they headed back north. Her condo remained as she left it. Unfortunately she was not lucky enough to have the electricity restored.

"Harry?" She asked the older frail gentleman who served as security for the front desk. "When do you think the power will be back on?"

"There was a young fellow here working on it about thirty minutes ago. He said it would be tomorrow sometime. But you young folks shouldn't complain. It's easy for you to take the stairs."

"Thanks Harry." Mayla smiled at the old man.

Harry must be in his eighty's. He was very thin and wore big glasses. Most doubted he could ever stop anyone from entering the building, but he was very friendly and could more than likely dial 911 if he had to.

They departed from Mayla's ocean front condo.

"We should stop by Shelby's house." Mayla said sitting next to Tom in his convertible. The sun had come out just as it was about to disappear in the horizon. Night was falling. The hurricane left a cool breeze behind. It was such a lovely evening. So surreal. It's hard to believe that less than five hours ago the winds were topping eighty miles an hour.

As they arrived at Shelby's home it was dusk, as the sun had gone to sleep. Her home was dark. Noticing the upstairs windows had been blown out with no attempt to clean the surrounding area, Mayla jumped from Tom's convertible before it was stopped. Turning to look at Tom as she sensed something was wrong. She was tense.

"I don't have a good feeling Tom." She shouted back to him as he opened his door.

"Maybe you should wait here."

"No, I'm fine."

Tom and Mayla stood banging on the front door for several minutes. There was no answer.

"Let's go around back." Tom lifted Mayla over the tall wooden fence that surrounded her back yard.

"Shit!" She said as she landed, "It's flooded. I'm all wet. Be careful Tom."

He pulled himself over, "I haven't much choice here now do I."

Mayla suddenly started screaming, "Ha! Tom! Something is crawling up my leg! Get it off! Get it off!"

Mayla actually frightened Tom. "Let me see." He lifted her pant leg to find a beetle has made its way up her leg. He brushed it off.

"You're alright."

She caught her breath. "Looks like we have some work to do here."

Mayla and Tom pried the plywood off one of the windows in the back of the house.

Tom lifted Mayla to the window as she peeked in.

"I can't see anything. It's too dark. It doesn't look like she has power either."

"I have a flashlight in my car, I'll go get it. I'll bring my cell phone too."

"What if the beetles?"

"Just scream again."

Tom returned with the flashlight and lifted Mayla to the window again.

"See anything?"

"There's water all over the floor! Try to call her again. If she doesn't answer her cell phone I think we should break in."

"What about her alarm?"

"No power. Besides, right now the police are not going to respond to a break in at house. Not now. Not after this hurricane."

Mayla dialed the phone while Tom looked for something to break the window. He knew she was not going to answer.

"Here, this will work." It was a hammer that had obviously gotten left behind after the installation of the make shift shutters.

"Stand back." Covering his head with his left arm and banging on the window with his right, Tom had knocked all the glass out of the frame. "Let me make sure there are no loose pieces left." He did not want Mayla to end up in the hospital getting stitches at his own carelessness. "I'll help you in, then come to the front door and let me in."

Mayla crawled though the window that led into the kitchen being careful not to touch any of the glass on the counter tops. The kitchen was clean. Almost like no one had been there for weeks. As Mayla jumped of the counter onto the floor she landed on a flooded kitchen floor. The water had to be about an inch deep.

Tom and Mayla would have never gone to Shelby's house if she would have just answered her telephone. If she went to her mothers or another friends house she would have brought her cell phone. Shelby had to stay in touch with her friends and family.

"Jeez." Chills were sent up her spine, as she was afraid to walk into the living not knowing what she may find. The flashlight bounced off the walls as she walked through the kitchen towards the living room. Everything was in place except for the water on the floors.

It wasn't Shelby's silver Tiffany key ring that sat under the mirror that caught Mayla's attention; it was the cell phone that sat next to them. Her heart sank. "Oh god." Mayla picked up the phone and shined the flashlight on the display.

"Nine missed calls. Oh god." Her voice became shaky. She knew Shelby was in the house. Mayla's eyes began to well up. She knew something wasn't right. She unlocked the front door and opened it for Tom.

"I don't want to look any further. Something is wrong. Her keys are here. Her cell phone is here too."

Tom walked through the front door looking around the townhouse at the same time.

"She has nine missed calls Tom."

"I see. Put that back where you got it."

Mayla put the phone back on the stand with the marble top.

"Wait here." Tom said.

"I don't want to wait by myself."

Mayla followed closely behind Tom holding the back of shirt as she looked from side to side as they walked up the stairs.

"Shelby! It's Tom and Mayla! Are you here?" Tom was calling through the house.

"Shelby." Mayla sang, "You home?"

"Are you all right? We let ourselves in. I can send Mayla home if you're naked!"

He felt a jarring sensation in his ribs as Mayla punched him for saying such a thing. The water was everywhere.

"Go to her room. It's over there to the right."

The almond colored hallway leading to her room had been stripped of the angel pictures that used to hang there. It was very difficult to see much else.

Tom slowly turned the brass handle to open the door to Shelby's bedroom. The remainder of the evening had barely given off enough light in the bedroom for them to notice the destruction of the hurricane. Shelby's suitcase next to the bed on its side as it had not been unpacked. It hasn't even been opened. Mayla began to cry as she scanned her room. Clothes strung out on the floor. Perfume bottles broken open. Pictures of her family lie face down on the wet tile.

Mayla moved close to Tom as they turned towards the bathroom. Grabbing his arm as they passed through the door.

"Shelby?" Tom called. "You here?"

There was no answer. The only sound you could hear was the wind blowing through the broken windows in the bathroom.

"Oh god Shelby!" Mayla cried as they came around the corner that led into her bathroom. Tom turned his head trying to fight back his own tears. He hadn't know anyone to die since his brother so many years ago. He felt a similar shock shoot through his body as when he found out about his brother. He couldn't fall apart in front of Mayla. He chose to remain strong.

Mayla fell next to the bathtub where Shelby's white naked body lies. She was cold and stiff, silent and lifeless. Her blood had hardened on her face leaving small traces in her hair. With her eyes closed she was still a beautiful girl.

Tom held Mayla for several minutes as she sobbed in his arms. After gathering herself she knelt next to Shelby's limp body stroking Shelby's hair with her fingers. Wanting to wash the blood from her face.

"She would never want anyone to see her like this."

"You need to leave her like she is." Tom stood behind Mayla caressing her shoulder. "I'll call."

He didn't say whom he would call. 911? The police? Her family? Her parents? What about her little sister? How will they handle what has happened to Shelby? Who will tell them?

The ambulance and police arrived a few minutes after the Tom called. The flashing lights blue and red lights bounced off the trees and the front of Shelby's town house. Neighbors and spectators emerged to see the commotion. Yellow police tape circled the home. An hour later, after pictures had been taken, after Tom, Mayla, and the neighbors were interviewed, Shelby was stuffed in a blue bag and brought her to the Broward County corners office for an autopsy.

"Why are they doing this to her? She doesn't need to be cut open and picked apart and probed at." Mayla asked Tom.

"She died alone. They have to."

Her family was notified. Camera crews from the television stations arrived. All standing out on the front lawn broadcasting "live" airing a death of a beautiful young girl who was employed at Max, Devon and Wheeler, a prestigious law firm in downtown Ft. Lauderdale. It was food for them. Exciting. The media. They thrive on misery. Loss.

It would be two o'clock in the morning before people would finally leave the front lawn.

CHAPTER SEVENTEEN

It was the morning after the discovery of Shelby's body. It was rather cool for a day in August. In the low eighties. The sun shined brightly on the front door of Shelby's home as it had only began to rise. A familiar noise from the distance began to draw near. Rumbling, noisy, muffled motor car. Sporty, not junky. It made a turn at the end of the block. As it became closer, the car revealed its color. Black. A shiny black. It was Robert. He drove slowly past her home. Heart beating with a saddened face. Anxiety built up inside him and turning his head as he slowly passed by. Looking lifeless in the home, he did not stop.

Instead he returned home to have lunch with Neddie and their daughter Francis.

"Here we are. Egg salad, no onions." Neddie said as she placed the sandwich in front of Robert.

"Thank you."

They sat quietly as they politely ate their egg salad and munched on some chips with their eyes glued to the television.

"I'm sorry all we can watch is the news Robert."

"I don't mind. Let's see what these reporters can dwell on." He hated the media. He wished they could simply report what was important and get on to another topic.

"No word yet on the cause of death with Shelby Peterson who was found last night in her home by two friends who had grown worried about her." The television blared. Robert heard about Shelby's death as he was lifting a sandwich to his mouth. His eyes grew big and began to water before he could excuse himself.

"Robert are you alright?"

"I'm fine." He stood and turned to quickly hide the tears that were about to take over his face. In the powder room he held his head in his hand and began to weep.

"I could have prevented this. If only she wouldn't have left me. Why did she anger me? Why did she threaten me? None of this would have happened. We could still be in London."

Robert tried to regain his composure by slapping cold water on his face. After blotting his face dry with the ivory colored towel, he examined his eyes in the mirror to see if they were red.

"Are you okay?" Neddie asked as he left the powder room.

"I choked a bit. I'm fine." He replied as he looked at his watch, "Look at the time. I need to get to the office. I promised the Mr. Collier from London that I would get some documents to him. I told him that I would have faxed them as soon as I got home but with this hurricane it simply slipped my mind."

Robert scrambled as he made his way out of the house. He had no intention of going to the office. He just had to leave his house and find somewhere private to go where he could learn more about Shelby's death. Zooming through the streets he ended up just where he had told his wife he would be. At the office.

He sat looking out his office window that overlooked Hollywood Boulevard. He did not pick up the phone to call anyone nor did he find a television or radio to listen to. He just sat with a blank look on his face staring over Hollywood Boulevard. It would be several hours before he left.

A few people straggled into the law office including Tom, Michael and Mayla. Max Simoni flew down in the afternoon to survey the damage and send his condolences to the family and friends of Shelby

Peterson. There was no damage to the office. The entire staff remained numb to the death of Shelby. The mood in the office was somber. Shelby's office door was opened with a few scattered pieces of paper on her desk. Just as she left it. Kenny and Julia stood in her doorway. That was the first time anyone would see a soft side to Julia. No one had any idea she actually cared for Shelby. Mayla would not be so hard on Julia after she had witnessed her tears.

"You ready to leave?" Tom asked Mayla as he poked his head into her office and noticing she had tears in her eyes. The last few days they had spent together had been very challenging, hurricane Gunther, and the loss of a good friend and coworker. "Hey." He said as he approached her closing the door behind him, "What's up there?" He placed his hand on her back as she put her head down and began to cry uncontrollably.

"Robert was married! The damn bastard was a married man! You need to hear the message. I can't imagine how she felt. She said she was going to call and tell his wife. She left him in London, not because of the hurricane, but because he was married."

Tom continued rubbing her back until she calmed down. "I want you to stay with me for a while Mayla. At least a week. I can't leave you alone. Vermin can stay too. Come on; let me get you out of this place. You've had enough for today."

Despite the horrible news of Shelby's death, Max would spend the night in town and take Michael and Marlene out to dinner in Palm Beach at the Breakers Hotel. It suffered no damage to its lush green landscaping.

Sipping hot tea Tom had made her. Her cell phone rang. "I can't answer that Tom, would you?" Mayla asked.

"Hello? Tom answering Mayla's cell phone. May I help you?"

He was trying to be very up beat and perky.

Tom's face grew white when the voice on the other end spoke.

"I see. How." He was interrupted. "What can I do?" He would pause again.

"But I don't understand. How could that possibly;" Interruption, pause.

"We have your number Mrs. Peterson." Pause again. "Wait!" The line went dead. Tom stood holding the phone in his hand.

"What's happened?" Mayla asked.

He did not respond.

"Tom, what did Mrs. Peterson want? Did it have to do with the funeral?"

"No."

"What then?" Mayla was prying. "Tom what happened? What is it?"

He sat down next to her on the sofa taking her tea from her and placing it on the table in front of her. "Mayla, Shelby was murdered."

"What? What are you talking about?" Her face wrinkled.

The corner's office had called Shelby's family and had explained the cause of her death had been drowning. There were small bruises around her neck and on her right shoulder. She had been dead three to four hours before the hurricane hit. There was water in her lungs."

"What? I never saw any bruises."

"Neither did I."

"I don't believe it."

"It's true Mayla. I don't know why anyone would want to hurt her."

The Broward County Sheriffs office had begun their investigation immediately and was contacting family members along with friends and ex-boyfriends.

"My god." Mayla said, as she remained numb to what she had just learned. "I think it may be Robert."

"What are you talking about?" asked Tom.

"The voicemail she left at work. I'll let you listen to it. She said Robert was a married man and she was going to call his wife to tell her. She was very upset. Maybe he took that as a serious threat."

"Did you archive her message?"

"Yes." Mayla hugged a pillow that sat next to her.

"We need to call the Sheriffs office. But do you really think he was capable of killing her?"

"He had much to lose Tom."

"We'll call them, but I think we should tell her family first."

"When?"

"I know it's not a good time, but we'll tell them after the funeral."

"I guess it would be best if we waited until then." Mayla agreed.

CHAPTER EIGHTEEN

It was the morning of Shelby's funeral. It wasn't raining that day. The church was lined with family and friends. Everyone from Max, Devon and Wheeler had shown up as they closed the office for the day. Most people were dressed in dismal black. Mayla stood close next to Tom's side occasionally leaning on him for support. They grew closer. Tom's demeanor was dim, as he had lost a good friend and co-worker.

Robert sat alone in a pew by himself. Sitting in the back row, he wore a black suit. Never looking up to the priest as he spoke. No one knew who he was, or did they ask.

Marlene, Michael and Max sat a row behind Tom. Marlene being the emotional person she is held a tissue close to her eye. Michael was silent. Max stood straight. His shiny baldhead reflected the lights from the ceiling above. He was making an impression for the firm. It was the right thing to do he thought; to fly to Ft. Lauderdale for the funeral; after all she worked for the firm almost three years before she was murdered.

Shelby's parents sat in the front pew along with the rest of the family. Her mother was wearing a long black dress with embroidered lace around the hemline. She would occasionally burst into tears as Mr. Peterson held her tightly with his left arm and hiding his tears with his right hand. Her sister Brigette's head never left the lap of her grandmother. She could not stand to see her sister lying in front of her loved ones, lifeless.

Shelby lay peacefully in her ivory colored casket. White roses surrounded her. The blood that was crusted on her face had been replaced with pancake make-up and blush. Blond curls surrounded her face. Her lips were pink. The casket had covered the lower part of her body. It was not Shelby at all. Not the lively girl everyone knew. It did not seem right. To just lie there. No life. How can there be a body without breath? Without a simple gesture. A twitch. Anything?

A woman sang a very powerful *Amazing Grace* from the balcony that echoed throughout the church. Shelby's favorite song. She used to sing it in the shower when she lived at home. She thought she sounded good.

After the funeral a reception was held at Mrs. Peterson's home. The house was crowded with relatives and friends of Shelby's. Some friends were from college and others from high school. Everyone brought cards and food. Occasional Mrs. Peterson would force a smile in order to thank people for coming to show their respects.

"Mr. Peterson," Tom asked with Mayla standing by his side, "We'd like to talk to you."

"About?"

"Shelby."

"I don't think this is the time or place."

"You may be interested in what we have to tell you Mr. Peterson, please."

Mayla spoke.

"We thought of calling BSO, but I thought you may like to hear this first." Tom intercepted the conversation.

"What is Tom?" He asked as if he were annoyed.

"I think we may know who," He paused. "We think we may know who took your daughter's life."

Mr. Peterson glanced over at his wife as her friends and family was consoling her.

"Who? Who would do this? Why would they do this?"

"Your daughter flew home early from London, it wasn't because of the hurricane Mr. Peterson." Tom was almost afraid to continue, "Robert, the man she went to London with was married. She didn't know until she was over there. She left a message on Mayla's voice mail at the office. It was clear that she was very distraught."

"So you think Robert murdered my daughter?"

Mayla turned her head towards Mrs. Peterson trying to hold back her tears.

"We're not positive but, I would say there is a good probability that he did." Tom said sternly, "She threatened to tell his wife."

Mr. Peterson sighed. "I guess we need to call the police and we need to do it quickly or I will kill him myself."

Mrs. Peterson noticed her husband was upset.

"Honey?" She said as she looked at Tom and Mayla.

"Sandra, I don't think we should talk about this now." He tried to straighten himself up so she would not see his anger.

"No, I think we should. It has to do with my baby doesn't it?"

Sandra is almost a replica of Linda Carter. One Halloween she dressed as Wonder Woman. Today however, she was different. She carried heavy bags under her eyes and her never before noticed crow's feet were more prominent.

"Marv, I would like to know what is going on."

Tom and Mayla remained silent.

"We think we may have an idea," he paused, "Who took our daughters life."

"Who?" She said frantically, "Tell me who? I want to know now!"

"Sandra please. Settled down."

"Don't tell me to settle down Marv! She's my daughter!"

"She my daughter too Sandra!"

Their voices grew loud as their guest began to stare at them.

"Mrs. Peterson," Mayla intervened and took Sandra's hand, "We think Robert killed Shelby. We're not sure but, well." She hesitated to continue, "He is a married man."

"Shelby would never!"

"She didn't know this until she got to London. She flew home early for what we thought was the hurricane. Yesterday I checked my voice-mail at work and she had left a message on it. She said she was going to tell Robert's wife."

"We're not certain, but we believe that he might be a suspect." Tom said.

"Oh God. She was falling in love with that man." She held Marv's arm tightly. "That bastard!"

"Honey."

"I don't give a damn! I want you to call BSO now!" Her eyes grew big, as she became more demanding.

"Honey, let's wait till our guests leave. Please. Calling now won't bring her back to us."

"As soon as the last person leaves? No. I want you to call them now!" Sandra picked up the cordless phone and handed it to her husband.

Michael saw the commotion in the corner and asked Tom what was going on.

"We think we may have a suspect."

"For?" Michael asked.

"Shelby."

"Oh." Michael seemed surprised, "How could you have a suspect?"

"Shelby called Mayla from London. Seems Robert is married and Shelby threatened to tell his wife."

"Ah poor Shelby." He sighed, "Are you sure?"

"No."

"Hardly a reason to kill anyone." Michael said with raised eyebrows.

"He's got a lot to lose."

"How is that Tom?" Michael tucked his hands in his pocket.

"Easy. He is a multi-millionaire."

"So."

"So his wife gets half of his money if he's found with a mistress. Maybe she's a tough woman. Think of what he would have to pay his attorneys." Tom sipped his coffee.

"Has anyone placed a call to BSO?"

"Mr. Peterson is going to if he hasn't already."

"Keep me informed Tom." Michael slapped Tom's shoulder then returned to his earlier conversation.

The Sheriffs department arrived shortly after Mr. Peterson called. Mayla had played the voice mail for the officer. It had been recorded and will be used as evidence in the case.

"We'll have to take Robert Edwards down for questioning." Detective Brian Henke said as he stood in the doorway. He was a tall man with blond hair cut so short you would have thought him to be bald. His eyes were like sapphires. He had a small-distinguished light colored mole above his lip. Shelby would have thought him to be a handsome man.

"Why can't you just arrest him now?" Sandra Peterson asked. "It's obvious he did it. No one has a reason to harm my baby." She was beginning to get upset again.

CHAPTER NINETEEN

Neddie was in the nursery with her daughter and Robert was in the study when the doorbell rang. With a dust rag in her hand, Maria the maid answered the door.

"Yes?' her Spanish accent was heavy, "May I help you please?"

"We would like to see Robert Edwards. Is he in?" asked detective Brian Henke.

"May I ask who you are?"

"Detective Brian Henke, Broward Sheriffs Office." He flashed his badge.

"One moment please."

"Who is it Maria?" Neddie asked as she walked down the stairs.

"Detective Brian Henke from Broward Sheriffs Office."

He flashed his badge again, this time at Neddie.

"What is it that you want with my husband?" She began to protect him.

"We just need to ask a few questions."

Robert walked out from his study with Maria the maid in tow.

"Yes sir?" Robert asked.

"I'm detective Brian Henke BSO. This is detective Mark Williams. We need to ask you a few questions about Shelby Peterson."

Neddie looked at Robert, "Shelby Peterson? Isn't she the girl that was murdered?"

"Yes ma'am." Detective Henke responded, "We need to take you husband down to ask him a few questions."

"What are you talking about? Why do you need to speak to my husband about the murder of Shelby Peterson?"

The two detectives did not answer.

"Robert could you please answer me?" Neddie began to shift her eyes between the detectives and Robert. No one answered her.

"Aren't you out of your jurisdiction?" Robert became defensive, as he knew they were accusing him of murder.

"Mr. Edwards, if you should choose not to come with us now we will visit you in your office, which is in Broward County. And if you wish for us to visit you there, we will. But I'm not sure that you would not want to give your clientele a show. It's up to you."

"Robert can you please tell me what is going on?" Neddie look at him as she began to get angry. "Did you know the girl that was murdered?"

"I will explain to you later."

Neddie was left standing in the doorway with her head cocked to the side as Robert left with the gentleman in the back seat of a dark blue Chevrolet.

They went to the Broward County Sheriffs office where he was fingerprinted and would be interrogated for several hours about his relationship with Shelby Peterson.

He felt everyone starring at him as he was led to the small unusually bright room.

"Take a seat." Detective Henke said, "Would you like some coffee?"

"Sure."

Robert circled around the room examining the two-way mirror each time he passed by. Finally settling down he sat at the head of the table.

"I can't believe I am here. I never imagined something so horrific like this would happen to me. What will happen to my business? My family? Neddie will kill me when I have to explain to her what I have done.

About twenty minutes later, Detective Henke and Williams returned to begin their questioning.

"How long have you known her? What were you doing in London together? You were spotted at her home the night of the murder, why were you there?"

There was a knock on the door to the small gray room that had a table with four chairs.

"Ya." Detective Williams asked.

A young woman opened the door. She was dressed in navy blue pants and a navy blue nylon jacket that had large yellow letters on the back that said BSO. She handed a paper to Detective Henke and spoke, "They match." She left the room without looking at Robert.

"Love that DNA stuff." Robert smirked.

"This isn't funny pal, a neighbor saw you outside her home on the night she was murdered. Did you not pull up in a yellow taxi? Your fingerprints are all over her house, on her front door, on the furniture, they're everywhere!"

"I need my lawyer."

"Yes you do." Williams said.

"I was in love with Shelby." Robert leaned into the table propping his arms up in front of him, "I told her I was married when we were in London. She got angry with me and left. I couldn't stop her. I thought I would wait until I moved out of the house to explain everything to her, I couldn't wait. She was so upset when she left I went to her house as soon as I landed. There was no answer so I left and went home. I figured she went to a friends house because of the hurricane."

"Would you like to wait for your attorney before you say anymore?" Detective Henke asked.

"I'll wait for my attorney. Can I go home now?"

Williams nodded at Henke and shrugged, "Don't plan on going anywhere."

"Where am I gonna go? I'm sure you'll be watching every move I make."

It was several hours later when Robert opened the front door to his home. Neddie was pacing near the foyer with the telephone in her hand.

"What is going on?" She asked, "What have you done?"

"Sit down Neddie." He pointed to the overstuffed antique chair that sat near the front door.

"Robert, tell me now!"

"Please sit."

She sat and he knelt down in front of her.

"I know we had an agreement." He held her hand. "I failed to live up to my end of the deal."

"What agreement would that be Robert?" She asked, as she was afraid to find out the truth.

"That we would wait to see anyone until the house in Boca was done."

Neddie stood as she began to get angry.

"Please Neddie, you need to let me finish. This is very important and you need to hear this."

"What? What do I need to hear? That you could not wait just one more month before you found someone?" She began to cry. "You are a terrible man!"

Robert moved close to hold her as she pushed him away. "Get a way from me!" She pushed him. She was hurt. She was not ready to hear the inevitable. Robert had met someone so quickly. He was going to tell her that he had to leave because he was in love with her.

"Neddie please listen to me!" He began to beg. "This is very important."

She sat back down on the over stuffed chair and let him speak.

"I met someone. Her name, "He spoke calmly before she interrupted him.

"You bastard! I knew it!" she stood and began to hit him out of embarrassment. "You couldn't wait?"

"Neddie calm down!" He grabbed her hands and began to push her towards the chair to sit her down. "Let me finish! I am in trouble! I need you! I need you to listen to me! We could lose everything!"

The desperation in his voice made her sit back down.

Robert began to speak again as tears fell from her eyes.

"I met a woman about three weeks ago. I brought her to London with me."

The tears came faster. She turned her head away from him because she did not want to see his face.

"Her name is Shelby Peterson. She was murdered. I am a suspect."

"Oh my god." She shrieked, "What did you do?" Neddie stood and began to pace around the room by the front door as her sobbing got louder and more intent.

"Well did you?"

"Never! Neddie how could you ever think I would do that to anyone! Never!"

"Then why are?"

Robert cut her off.

"When we were in London I told her I was married. She never knew. She left a message on a friend of hers voicemail at work. She threatened to call you."

"Oh god." Neddie held her head in her hands and continued to cry as Robert finished speaking.

"I let her leave London because she was so angry with me. I thought it best for me not to chase after her. I would call on her after I moved out. I had already messed things up so badly. I've lied to you and I've lied to her."

Neddie could not stop crying. She was in disbelief. "Did you love her?"

"I was falling in love with her. She was a wonderful girl. I just got carried away and invited her to London with me."

"You just couldn't wait, could you? Now you see what you have done?" Neddie was very distraught. She felt anger, sadness and finally an end to her marriage.

"I'm sorry I have hurt you. There will be much more for us to deal with. I'm so sorry I drug you and Francis into this."

"I'm so embarrassed by your actions Robert. I don't know what to do."

"I'm sorry."

"Did you kill her?"

"Never. You know me better than that."

Within hours of Robert's return home, newscasters sat outside the gated community he lived in. His name would be ruined along with his business, as he would be the breaking story at ten o'clock.

"You see that?" Michael said to Marlene as he stood in front of his television. "Didn't take them long to get that bastard."

"What are you talking about?" she said wiping her hands with a towel as she walked from the kitchen.

"This guy Shelby went to London with. Look what they are calling this! London lovers! This damn station. Kick them when they're down. London lovers. Give me a break."

"Have you heard anything else at work?"

"No. They are trying to pin the murder on him. There is no one else that would want to hurt that girl."

"Yes. You are right. Shelby was sweet."

Michael remained standing in front of the television as Marlene finished doing the dishes from dinner.

CHAPTER TWENTY

Slowly the firm would regain it's daily routine. Michael didn't want to hire a new secretary to replace Shelby. It was too soon. He would have Mayla help him out here and there. Sometimes Marlene would come in and give a hand.

Robert still remained a suspect in the murder case.

Tom prepared himself for the Riley case, as it was about to go to trial in another week. Mayla stood close by to assist him. They continued to spend time with each other.

"Hey." It was Tom standing in the doorway to Mayla's office. "What are you doing?"

"Just looking over these stories for the Riley case. Are you about ready for this thing?"

"Just a few finishing touches and we'll be good to go."

"Have we ever heard anything else about the break in that we had?" Mayla seemed curious as she held a pencil to her mouth and sat back in her chair.

"We think it may be kids."

"I see." She said.

"Your office is a mess. I've never seen it like this before."

"I'm well aware of its condition."

"Mayla, would you like to go to happy hour tonight? Or better yet, let's have dinner. I'll take you somewhere nice."

"Sure." Mayla remained dazed.

"Everything okay with you?"

"I'm fine." She sat up in her chair, "Seems BSO thinks Robert murdered Shelby huh?"

"I'm sure he did. Why would anyone else have a reason?"

"Hmm." She agreed.

"Shall I pick you up?"

"Sure. Where are we going?"

"I think Chez Pierre would be nice."

"Wow. Chez Pierre?"

"You need a good meal and bottle of some fancy French wine, or champagne. What ever you want." Tom smiled. "I'm just the guy to fill that order."

"Well in that case, why don't you pick me up. I'll feel like a Cinderella." She waved her hands in the air.

"I'll be at your house at six-thirty."

"So early?"

"Yes. I thought we could have a cocktail and watch the sunset over downtown."

"You know that view is out of my bedroom." She smiles as her eyes peeked above her shyness.

"Well then," he said, "We can watch the seagulls on your balcony."

"That will be fine."

The doorman called Mayla to announce the arrival of Tom. She opened the door to greet him. He handed her flowers.

"These are for you miss." He bowed.

"These are lovely. Thank you Tom."

"Flowers can really brighten up a room. I thought these past couple of days have been so hard on you that you could use them."

"Your right, I can. Why don't you make us a cocktail while I put these flowers in some water? Say hello to Vermin, he's been asking about you."

As Mayla walked to the kitchen Tom could help but notice how she swept her hair on top of her head. The black skirt she was wearing came to the top of her knees. He thought it was so sexy because of the slits on the front where here thighs would peek out as she walked. Her gray cashmere sweater had three quarter length sleeves with tiny beads and embroidery around the neckline.

"Stunning." Tom whispered to himself.

"Have you seen the news lately?" Mayla called from the kitchen; "They are calling Shelby's case the Affair of the London Lovers. Isn't that pathetic?"

"Ya." Tom was pouring a small amount of gin into some short crystal glasses and tossing an olive in each.

Mayla returned from the kitchen with her flowers neatly arranged in a vase.

"They are beautiful Tom. Thank you. It helped."

"My pleasure. Anything for the lovely Miss Martin." He bowed again.

"Anyway, when I got home tonight I turned on the television and there was channel seven standing outside our office building. You may not have to wait until the Riley trial to get all the publicity you want."

He handed her the cocktail.

"Gin. Warm gin. Hope you like it. I'm sure we are going to be the talk of the town for quite some time."

Mayla opened the door to her balcony that overlooked the Atlantic Ocean. There were two wrought iron chairs out there along with a small round table. Tom sat down.

"You can't see the seagulls if you are sitting. The railing is in the way."

"Maybe I don't want to see the birds."

Mayla knew he was making a reference to her bottom. Tom stood and leaned on the railing with her.

"Nice view." He said.

"Amazing isn't it? I have traffic and tall buildings on one side of my house and on the other, pure serenity. I like it. It's peaceful and it helps me unwind after a hectic day."

"Maybe I should borrow your balcony once and a while."

"Anytime." Mayla sipped her drink. "Anytime you want."

Robert spent most of his time with his attorney and a private investigator that Neddie suggested. She thought perhaps there was a part of Shelby's life that she did not share with Robert and a private investigator would not be as biased as the Sheriffs office would on convicting him. The private investigator, Randy Hunter will trace the last few weeks of Shelby's life. Neddie decided to put her two cents in after reading a report in the newspaper.

"Making me money or not, I will do no business with such a man." One stuffy old woman quoted to the Sun-Sentinel.

Even though Robert had lied to her about his affair with Shelby, she believed he did not kill her. She knew him too well, for too long and watching him with bags under his eyes, unable to eat, she began to feel sorry for him.

"Robert." Neddie said as she approached him at his desk in the study, "If you need to sell the house in Boca and stay here a bit longer you can."

"No." He replied as he raised his head above his computer, "I've caused enough problems in your life right now. I don't want to complicate things more."

"I offered." She said as she stood there with her hands by her side.

"Thank you."

"Robert, please don't embarrass me like that again."

"I don't think there is anything in the world that I could do to you that would cause you more pain than I already have." He removed his glasses from his face.

Neddie walked closer.

"Yes you can."

"Can what?"

"Cause me more pain." She said as she sat on the dark brown leather chair in front of his desk.

"How could I possibly?" He seemed puzzled.

"Did you kill her?" Neddie dusted a picture of her daughter as she asked.

"I thought you believed me."

"I do, but you did lie to me about her."

"Neddie please, don't start with me. I told you everything. I need your support! I'm at wits end here. I'm about to lose my business, some of my staff have quit, I'm being charged with murder, you should know that I would never harm anyone that I care," he stopped himself.

"Care about." Neddie finished the sentence as she felt a slight sting in her heart. Her eyes watered.

"I'm sorry." He said.

"I guess I'm not as strong as I thought I was. Sorry to have bothered you."

"Neddie," he stood, "come here."

She walked to him where he embraced her as she cried. She knew no one else could hold her the way he did. She snuggled her face into his chest.

"Really, I am so sorry I have caused you such a great deal of pain. Maybe you should back away from this. Go somewhere with your sister. It will be my treat."

"No. I can't leave now. The authorities will surely think you are guilty if I am running away."

Neddie stepped back from Robert; "Maybe I can help you."

"You already have."

"No Robert. You need to try and remember every step you took after leaving the airport. Every tiny step. Try to remember everyone you came in contact with."

"I remember the guy who picked me up from the airport. He was Jamaican."

"Did you get his name?" She asked.

"Of course not."

"How about the taxi company?"

"It was Yellow Miami. I remember because of all the palm trees on their cars. I always thought them to be so silly."

"Those silly palm trees may have just saved you life in prison."

"Do you have any idea how many Jamaican taxi drivers there are in Miami?"

"It won't be that difficult Robert. Just find out who was working that night. I'm sure they keep all their records. If you can get a hold of this guy and he remembers you, and where he took you, that will be your way out."

"I will start now. I will call the Yellow Miami Taxi myself. Then I need to call that P.I. I hired, Randy Hunter. I'll let him work on it."

Neddie reached for a tissue on the back of Robert's desk and dried her face.

"Something so simple. Thank you Neddie."

She left the room.

Robert sat back down in his chair and dialed directory assistance.

"Yes, in Miami. Yes the number for Yellow Miami Taxi." He paused with his Monte Blanc pen in his hand, "Thank you. Thank you very much."

He began to write. Hanging up the phone, then dialing again he felt he had a small tinge of hope.

"Mr. Hunter?" Robert spoke into the headset, "Robert Edwards here. Go earn the money I pay you. I want you to question all the Jamaican taxi drivers who work at Yellow Miami Taxi. I want you to find out the name of the driver who took me to Shelby's house on the night she was murdered. He is my ticket to freedom."

"Dinner was wonderful!" Mayla said to Tom, "Thanks for lifting my spirits."

"My pleasure, as always." He opened the car door for her and walked around to his side.

Mayla looked at him as he put the key in the ignition, "How are you doing Tom?"

"Good thanks."

"No Tom, please look at me. Are you okay? You're always trying to lift my spirits, how are you?"

Tom put his hand on her knee, "I'm just fine."

She held his stare. There was silence as he felt weakness overcome him. He wasn't about to show his soft side. The death of Shelby had taken its toll on him along with the pressure of the Riley case.

"You sure?" She asked again.

"I'm sure."

He put the car in reverse and back out of his spot, "I can't believe that place didn't have a valet."

"That would have been the perfect moment for a kiss." Mayla said to herself. *"What is his problem. Now I have no one else to talk to this about. Shelby? Can you hear me? I know you're up there. What is his problem? Why hasn't he tried to kiss me? Maybe he doesn't think I'm attractive."*

Mayla sighed.

"Alright?" Tom looked to Mayla as they sat at the light on Federal and Broward.

"Yes."

His scent drifted over towards her as he gripped the steering wheel with his left hand.

Mayla began to take deep quiet breaths of air trying to hold herself back. The wine had gotten to her.

"Damn french men." She thought.

"Do you have a busy day tomorrow?" Tom asked.

"I really need to clean up my office. It's a mess."

"I'll need you to help me tomorrow. Can it wait another day?"

"Sure."

Tom parked his car outside the entrance to her condo while he walked Mayla to her front door.

"Thanks again for dinner Tom. I had a great time."

"So did I." He leaned in towards her cheek and kissed her softly. "Good night."

Chapter Twenty-one

It was early the next morning and the maid was serving oatmeal with fresh fruit and yogurt for breakfast when the phone rang.

"I'll get it." Maria the maid said as she put a bowl of oatmeal in front of Neddie.

"Hello? Yes. He cannot come to the phone at the moment. May I take a message?" Maria had been instructed to never interrupt any meal or sleeping time for a phone call. "Yes Mr. Hunter. I will tell him."

Robert perked up when he realized it was Randy Hunter the private detective.

"Maria," Robert asked, "What did he say?"

"To call him right away. He said he has good news for you."

Robert looked across the table at Neddie as he shoveled hot oatmeal into his mouth.

"Good news. Did you hear that?"

"I heard that." She smiled.

"I hear too daddy." Francis slammed her fists on her high chair. The adorable little girl had oatmeal in her brown curly hair and on her rosy cheeks.

"I don't think I can wait to call him."

"Relax Robert. Have your breakfast then call him."

Neddie remained calm.

"Just a few more bites." After wiping his mouth with a cloth napkin he stood and walked quickly towards the phone and dialed Randy Hunter.

"Randy, it's Robert Edwards. I understand you have some good news to tell me."

He let out a brief laugh. "I see. You did. And what did he say?" Robert would occasionally pause. "Thanks Randy. I owe you a round of golf and then some."

Robert hung up the phone and turned to Neddie, "He found the taxi driver that took me to."

Neddie gave him a look as she stood to clear her plate.

"I'm sorry. I keep screwing things up. I keep hurting you. Neddie, I think maybe I should leave sooner. With everything that's going on around here I just keep hurting you. I can't do this to you anymore." He felt truly saddened when he saw the look on her face.

"Maybe you should." She agreed as she turned her back towards him.

"I'll find a place today. Maybe I will call my mother and see if I can stay with her until the house is done."

Neddie said not another word to him for the rest of the morning.

Robert phoned his mother from his study.

"Hello Mom. How are you?" He said shortly after dialing her number. And so it would be. Robert would leave Neddie that afternoon.

He was upstairs packing his clothes when Neddie walked into what used to be their room.

"Hi." He said in a glum voice as he put some jeans in a suitcase. "I'll get the rest at another time. I'll call before I bother you."

"Neddie sat on the hand sewn quilt that was on the queen sized bed. "You're not a bother. But it would be easier." Tears trickled down her cheek as Robert came to her side.

"I'm sorry it didn't work between us Neddie. I will always love you. You're the mother of a wonderfully amazing little girl. I thank you for helping me bring her into this world. I will do anything I can for you to make this separation easier."

Neddie sobbed as Robert held her at the end of their bed that they once shared.

"Can I tell you why I feel so terrible Robert?"

"Please."

"In a way I feel responsible for the death of this girl."

"Are you crazy?" He pulled her chin up to look at her eyes, "How could you possibly think that?"

"You could have been with her if you weren't here with me."

"Neddie, please. It is what it is."

He held her for several minutes rocking her to comfort her.

"I will call you to make sure you're okay and to say good-night to my little girl."

"I'll be fine Robert. But how are you? There's no denying you were falling in love with this girl. I can't even say her name, it hurts too much. We haven't been in love in so long and to be honest with you, if a man were to have approached me in the state we were in, I may have accepted. Love is such a wonderful thing."

"I will be fine."

Deep inside Robert did everything he could to keep his feelings hidden from Neddie.

Neddie hugged Robert inside the garage before he left. Her tears had dried up and she was going to stay with her sister for a few days.

Robert called Detective Williams and Henke to prove his innocence and had asked them to follow through with the investigation.

"Well to be honest with you Mr. Edwards," said Henke, "She had tissue samples under her fingernails and they didn't match yours."

"How could it take you so long to figure that out? I have been humiliated by the entire state of Florida! My business is going from bad to worse, I have lost employees and I'm being publicized as the London Lover! I can't go anywhere without a finger being pointed at me or worse yet, my family! And to top it off, someone murdered someone that I care very much about!"

"I understand Mr. Edwards. Things were slow because of the hurricane."

He slammed the phone down.

"Honey, what is wrong with you?" Robert's mother asked.

"I'm just so amazed at the way things are done. First, the media makes you out to be guilty as sin then when you are innocent there are no repercussions!"

Robert's mother was in her early seventies. She was a very tall woman. Not very typical of a South Florida senior citizen. Her hair was salt and pepper and she wore glasses from the early nineties. Her husband, Robert's father, lived somewhere in Alabama. He would surface on occasion when he needed something. Mrs. Edwards always obliged, as she was a good Christian woman.

"Let me get you some tea son."

And so she did.

The investigation would go slow as there were no other suspects in the case. Everyone from family to co-workers to ex-boyfriends of the past was questioned. No one else in the neighborhood saw any strange cars sitting outside her home just hours before hurricane Gunther struck. The detectives would lie low hoping for something, or someone to pop up.

All of South Florida had returned to normal, minus a few trees a week after Gunther hit.

Robert tried to salvage his business as a few customers decided to give the brokerage another chance. After all, most were happy with their personal broker. The few employees he had lost begged for their jobs back. He would not take them back as he thought them not to be loyal. Through thick and thin was his motto.

It hasn't rained in a few days. And in such a short time landscaping began to turn brown because of the heat.

CHAPTER TWENTY-TWO

"Hi honey." It was Michael calling his wife. He was in a great mood. "We have been invited to New York for dinner with Max."

He pushed his big leather chair away from his desk and looked out the window down to the street where construction workers were busy building another high rise office building.

"Yes honey. I understand that. Friday, we'll spend the night. Max's treat."

He saw a woman try to run through the rubble with her Boxer puppy.

"I'm not sure if he is going, but I know Max invited him also."

A construction worker came to her rescue. She seemed to be grateful. The man in the hard hat watched her walk off.

"I guess he's happy with all the publicity we have been receiving lately."

Michael held the phone away form his ear as Marlene's voiced shot right through the lines.

"Shame on you Michael! How dare you get excited over the loss of someone close to you! I will not go to New York for dinner with that evil, evil man!"

"But," Michael tried to speak, "Honey the publicity is from the Riley case. We start on Monday."

She went silent. "I'll go shopping for a new outfit today and ask mother to watch the girls."

"I love you when you get like that."

"You should love me all the time."

"I do."

"Bye." She hung up.

Mayla and Tom were in the conference room piecing together the Riley case.

"If I can get this guy eight years, I will be happy." Tom said as he bent over the twelve-foot bird's eye maple table.

"It's not like he killed anyone." Mayla said, "I know it's a terrible thing to say but it's true. He was only, well I guess he was trying to have someone murdered, kinda, kinda Castro."

"Well we know that is not what we will present to the jury. He was just trying to oust Castro by sending money to his wife's family. Too bad she's not fit to testify. She would have been a good one."

"We don't need her." Mayla added stapling papers together. "We have enough sympathy stories to get him a minimal sentence. Maybe even probation." Mayla began to laugh. "Maybe we can even get him his insurance license back!" It suddenly became a joke for them.

"Say," Tom asked, "Would you like to take a break before the trial?"

"What do you mean?" She looked around the room to locate her bottled water.

"Come to New York this weekend with me."

"Huh?" She looked puzzled.

"For dinner. Max has invited Michael and I because of all the publicity we have been getting. More attorneys are interested in working for our firm. That means more money for Max, Michael and me. We have been getting more requests for our services."

"Yes we have been getting a lot of attention because of the Riley case." Mayla responded as she gulped her water.

"Sure. I'll go. Are you going to buy me a new dress?"

"You want me to buy you a new dress?"

"Yes, I work hard. And besides, you do want me to look good don't you?"

Tom was amused by Mayla's request.

"And when will we do this?"

"After we finish here tonight."

"We'll be working late." He said.

"We can go at lunch time. Nieman Marcus at Galleria."

"What ever you want Mayla, you have been such a good little worker."

Mayla didn't mind the extra hours she had been putting in on the case. It took her mind off of Shelby and she enjoyed Tom's company.

"Matching shoes too?"

"Sure, why not."

"Handbag?"

"No."

"Fine."

They continued to work up until two before they broke for lunch. On the way out Tom signaled to Michael that he and Mayla would be going out for lunch. Michael waved him into his office.

"Ya?" He said as he checked his wallet for his credit card.

"I guess you will be bringing Mayla to New York?"

"Says who?"

"Max."

Tom smiled, "Yes."

"Is there anything going on?"

"Not yet. Need anything while we're out?"

"No thanks."

Tom turned and left. Michael sat back in his leather chair to review plans to expand the firm.

Mayla and Tom got drive-thru at Arby's on Sunrise Boulevard so they had time to spend at the mall. By the time they parked the car there were only a few fries that had to be eaten.

"Oh Tom, I just thought of something."

"What's that?" He said with a mouthful.

"If you are with me when I pick out the dress, you will see the dress and it won't be a surprise."

"What are you trying to say?"

"That it won't be a surprise Tom." Mayla flashed him a look like he was dense.

"So you want to surprise me, and show me how beautiful you are in the dress I am buying for you?"

Mayla was embarrassed when she realized that he had found out her little secret. She wanted to look nice for him. She wanted him to pay her a compliment when he saw her. She held her head down then perked it back up.

"Okay Busted! Is that so bad? I'm a woman and I like to be paid an occasional compliment every now and then."

After arriving at the mall, Mayla tried on several dresses before she settled on one. Tom had to turn his back as he paid for it. The young lady at the register was so amused by their behavior she had to ask if they were married. Tom responded, "Not yet."

After selecting her shoes, the trip to the mall had been concluded.

"You should have bought me a handbag Tom. I got the shoes on sale."

CHAPTER TWENTY-THREE

Tom, Michael, Mayla and Marlene were flown first class to New York that Friday late in the afternoon, compliments of Max, who would in turn use the trip as a tax write off. They were greeted by a limousine driver dresses in a black suit wearing a ponytail.

"Wheeler-Devon party?" He asked as the foursome approached.

"Yes." Tom answered.

The driver managed to handle the women's luggage. Tom and Michael had to fend for themselves.

"You'll be staying in the Waldorff. Max wanted you to be comfortable, so you will be in a suite. You will have time to freshen up and I will return to pick you up for dinner at seven-thirty this evening."

"Very nice." Mayla said to Marlene. "If we had time we could get a facial."

"See you kids in a couple hours." Michael nodded and smiled at Tom insinuating that he and Mayla would engage in some type of promiscuous act. Mayla did not see Michael's assumption. They left the elevator and went to their separate rooms.

"This is beautiful." Mayla's eyes scanned the room. The room was decorated with furniture form the late eighteen hundreds. "And where will you be sleeping this evening?"

"Wherever you would like me to. I am a gentleman." Tom hung his suit in the closet.

"Look at this Tom, it's a bottle of Dom!" Mayla removed the champagne from the bucket and held it up to Tom, "Do you think we can open it now?"

"If you like, however I don't want any misbehaving at dinner."

"Never!" Her eyes grew wide.

"Open it then."

"You open it. You're the man!" She demanded.

"Women." Tom took the green bottle from Mayla and peeled back the foil, "Stand back." He threatened as he released the cork into the air.

"Does Max know that you brought me?"

"Yes he does."

"Does he think we are?"

"Sleeping together?" Tom interrupted.

"I guess." She held the champagne glasses as Tom poured the bubbly into them.

"I have no idea. Quite frankly, I don't care."

"Cheers."

They drank nearly half the bottle before Mayla confessed that she was beginning to feel a bit tipsy.

"Hate to waste such a great bottle." She said

"We can always get another."

"Maybe later."

Mayla excused herself and went to take a shower to sober her up a bit. She emerged fresh and energized with a towel on her head and wearing a big white robe.

"Your turn."

Tom was taken back by Mayla when he saw her for the first time in the short yet elegant black beaded dress he bought for her.

"What an investment." He looked up and down at her slender body. "You really are a lovely woman."

"Thank you. Thank you for my dress. And my shoes." She giggled as she put on a show for him. Her scent danced around him as she spun.

"Magnificent." He said to himself.

"Your wearing glasses Tom." She stopped.

"I lost a contact."

"You look great in them."

Small wire rimmed glasses sat on the end of his nose. He looked over them to watch her as he sat back in a large wooden chair with ball and claw feet.

Mayla snuck another sip of champagne as he watched her. It was almost like the time he caught her with the chocolates in Shelby's office.

"Mother would like this one."

"Like what?" Mayla asked.

Caught off guard, "These chairs." Tom was quick to respond. "We should go."

"Good evening!" Michael and Marlene were already waiting in the lobby. "Mayla you look wonderful! And Tom you are handsome as ever."

Marlene and Mayla greeted each other with a kiss. It wasn't long before the Guido the limo driver would arrive. They were taken to Michelino's, a small Italian restaurant a few miles from the hotel. It was a difficult restaurant to get into but Max had his connections. The restaurant was very old Italy. Crown moldings with paintings on the ceiling mocking the Sistine Chapel in Rome.

Max stood unaccompanied waiting for them at the bar to the left of the front door. He never had a date with him. He was married several years ago but his wife had left him for another man. Max had become so involved with his work he had neglected any attention towards his wife. The divorce had broken his heart because he had wanted children so badly. Children that would carry on the family name. He never stopped loving Sophia. So if he ever had a date, it would be just that, a date. He was dressed in a dark suite with a celery colored Armani tie.

All smiles hugs and kisses were passed out. They were seated.

"I want to thank everyone for coming here this evening." Max raised his glass, "It has been a bumpy road and we have experienced a few trying moments, hurricane Gunther and mostly the loss of not only a co-worker, but a good friend to everyone at this table this evening." Max paused, "To Shelby."

Everyone toasted, sipped, and returned their glasses to the table.

It was a somber moment. There was silence. Max sat.

After dinner the gentleman went to the bar to have a cigar while Mayla and Marlene sat at a table talking about Marlene's children and the possibility of another. They sipped on Kaluha and cream.

"So tell me Tom," Max said as he leaned on the bar, "Think we'll get any more publicity from this case?"

"We'll see how much more we get, Monday is the big day." He replied.

"Are you ready for it?"

"Absolutely. It will be a total sympathy case. I'll have the jury crying on my opening argument. Shouldn't take long." He was cocky.

"I'm glad you are so confident." Max sipped his brandy; "May I help in anyway?"

"You already have you bastard, we're doing this for free. Give me my hourly salary." He thought before he spoke, "Nope. All set."

"Great, glad to hear it." He turned to Michael, "I know this is such a tough subject Michael, but has there been any news on Shelby?"

"We thought it was her boyfriend Robert Edwards but he had an alibi. They had to start over with nothing to go on except skin beneath her nails."

Tom removed himself from the conversation the gentlemen were having. He was busily focusing his attention on Mayla. She sat gracefully listening intently to Marlene speak. She smiled.

"If I may be of assistance. Please let me know. I have an excellent private detective. I can hire him to speed up the investigation."

"I don't think that will be necessary. But thank you Max."

Max took his last sip of brandy. "Well gentlemen, shall we call it an evening?"

"Sounds good." Tom stretched as he signaled the ladies that it was time to go.

"Tom," asked Max, "Why did you choose to bring Mayla?"

A smile overcame his face; "She needed a night out. We'll be leaving in the tomorrow afternoon. We need to work on Sunday."

The limo ride back to the hotel was quick. Michael and Marlene parted holding hands as they spun around the corner to their suite.

"There are such a great couple." Mayla said as Tom opened the door to the room. "Look at this! A fresh bottle of champagne. We'll have to open it! We can't bring it with us, it's already been chilled and it's a no no to let it grow warm."

He held the bottle up to Mayla, "Madam, champagne?"

"Please." She responded as she walked toward the window that over-looked the city lights.

"Here we are." Tom said as he approached her from behind.

"Lovely, isn't it?" Mayla said as she did not move.

"Soon there will be snow falling from the sky."

"The streets will be wet."

"The city will be decorated with lights."

The conversation was monotone as they envisioned the city in a few months. Tom retrieved the champagne bottle that sat chilling on the round cherry table. He returned in slow motion with the bottle in his left hand, his glass in the right. Her scent lingered through the air over towards him. Her hair pinned up exposing her bare neck seem too temptatious for him to resist. On his slow approach he tilted his head so slightly, examining the small brown mole just under her hairline and pressed his lips against it. She moved ever so slightly, just enough for him to continue as she did not resist. Chills ran up and down the small of her back. He kissed her mole several times before he would work his way to her lips that were laced with champagne and color. The kiss so soft, he held his mouth there and did not retrieve nor did he press for more. An artist could sculpt the moment.

"I like the snow." Tom said after pulling away.

It ended there. They slept in the same bed.

The following morning was embarrassing for them. Perhaps they have taken it too far. It was only an innocent kiss. Nothing more.

"I'm sorry if I offended you last night." Tom said in morning as he sat at the end of the bed as Mayla woke from her sleep.

"I'm not offended. Maybe it was the champagne."

"Maybe it wasn't."

"Maybe."

"Would you like to do any sight seeing before our plane leaves?"

"Sure," Mayla sat up and stretched, "Take me to the Statue of Liberty, I've only been there once."

"After breakfast then."

The flight home was awkward. Tom hadn't made a pass to Mayla all day. Maybe it was the champagne. No chance for a relationship here she thought. It was typical of Tom to love em' and leave em'. He was thinking quite the opposite. I've embarrassed her. She'll probably want to quit her job just as soon as the Riley case is over. They were very polite to each other on the plane.

CHAPTER TWENTY-FOUR

Sunday morning Tom picked Mayla up at her condo, took her to breakfast and then to the office to put the finishing touches on the opening statement. The Brothers to the Rescue director was contacted along with several Cuban American families. They worked from ten till three before they broke for some lunch.

"When we get back Mayla, I will need the file on the rafters."

"Yes sir."

"Where would you like to go for lunch?"

"The French restaurant."

"Sounds good."

Lunch was simple. A beautiful Sunday afternoon sitting outside watching the people enjoying their day, as they would stroll by with their dogs and their children. It made it difficult to return to work.

"How's the salmon?"

"Delicious. Your crepe?"

"Same." Tom paused as he thought he might approach Mayla with an awkward question, "Maybe after the trial Mayla, we could return to New York to finish out the weekend. Catch a show or something." Unable to look at her in fear of rejection he studied the creamy sauce that lay over the crepe.

"I think you will owe me that much."

"Great." He still didn't look at her.

"Tom, did you want to ask me out on a real date until then?" Mayla's face turned red due to her boldness.

He stopped staring at his plate and looked at Mayla, "Absolutely." His small dimples appeared on his cheeks as he finally had the courage to look at her. "This week we will have dinner."

"You better ask me three days in advance."

"What, now because I want to take you on a quote, real date, unquote, you follow the rules?"

"You know about the rules?"

"I am man of the new millennium. Of course I do."

"Then you should know, I'm a busy girl."

"You've been spending all your time with me."

"You won. When is our quote, real date, unquote going to be?"

The waiter stopped to check on them.

"Well?" She asked.

"Well what?" He asked.

"When?"

"This week."

"Give me a day."

"Don't be such a typical woman, it's why I liked you in the first place."

"Fine."

After lunch they returned to the office. Mayla went to her office to fetch the papers Tom had asked for.

"What a mess." She looked on her desk that she had not tended to for almost two weeks. "Where to begin?"

She started flipping through the stacks on her desk with the trashcan near by.

"Junk. Garbage. Old mail." Tossing them as she spoke.

"Ooh Victoria's Secret. Behave." Threw it in the trash.

"Hmm." It was a large white envelope. She opened it, as it had not been addressed. She hoped she had not forgotten to mail off some important documents. She carefully opened the envelope and slid the papers out. She began to flip through them, as they look unfamiliar to her. There was a list with names of people in various nursing homes throughout in South Florida. Several money orders were tucked between the papers.

"What the heck? I've never seen this before."

Having no idea what is was she continued to read further. "Looks like info for the Riley." She stopped. There was a letter.

Jim,

Enclosed you will find additional lists to be used. If you have any further questions please contact Max, or myself. I will expect your call upon receipt of this envelope.

Mike

It dawned on her that this was the envelope she was to deliver for Shelby but had forgotten to do so when she selfishly stole a piece of chocolate and it dripped on her new blouse.

"Oh my god." She realized these papers were from Michael. *What would he be doing with the evidence from the Riley case? Who was the envelope for? Does Tom know about this? Should I tell him? Mayla researched the names on of the people in the nursing homes.*

"None of these names look familiar. These can't be for the Riley case. As a matter of fact," she turned to look and see if Tom was looking over her shoulder.

"Oh God." Chills were sent up her spine, as she suddenly realized what she had gotten herself into. This was a list of names for persons that needed to be insured. *Could Michael be involved? Was he part of the Riley scam? Who is Mike? What about Tom? Is he aware of this? Is he involved also?*

"Mayla?" It was Tom. She quickly folded the envelope in half and stuffed it in her purse.

"Ya?" She called through the doorway.

"Do you have that file for me?"

"Yes, coming."

It was best to keep this envelope from him for now. How could she investigate this? Who will help her?

"Here we are." She said as she handed the file to Tom.

"You all right?"

"Yes, I think maybe lunch didn't agree with me."

"Well I hope you feel better. Can I get you anything?"

"No thanks, I'll be fine."

They continued to work for two more hours. Mayla tried hard to hide in her mind what she had discovered.

"Would you like to have dinner tonight?" Tom asked as he drove her home.

"I really don't feel well." Mayla said, "Tomorrow maybe."

"Sure."

Tom thought maybe she was trying to pull away from him.

"I won't give up so easily Miss Martin."

He drove off.

Mayla studied the contents of the envelope while sitting on her plush ivory sofa. She picked up the phone and began to dial the nursing homes to check and see if the people listed were in fact a resident. All of them had checked out to be so. One, Clara Brighton, had passed away. It was decidedly so, part of the insurance scam.

She realized that the Mike in the envelope was Michael. He was definitely involved in the insurance scam. But how? Why? Who could she turn to for help? What if Tom is involved? How will she face him in the morning? How could she face Michael? Ever? Then she began to ponder the thought that maybe this had something to do with the murder of Shelby.

Mayla sat on her balcony watching the seagulls flutter around the ocean looking for food. A little boy was with an older child feeding the birds popcorn. How nice it would be to be those children.

"Robert. I can contact Robert. He has been cleared of the murder. He can help, if he's willing."

Mayla searched through the phone book calling all of the Robert Edwards that had been listed. One number she called had been disconnected. She figured it to be him. He must have had it disconnected after the murder investigation. She continued to scan the pages of the phone book ruling out the obvious, calling all of the Edwards listed figuring someone had to know him. It took her an hour and a half to call all of Dade County. She continued her search in Broward County. A half-hour later, she spoke to an older woman named Constance.

"Yes he is here, shall I say who is calling?"

"My name is Mayla. Mayla Martin from Max Devon and Wheeler.

"One moment Mayla."

She rubbed her tired eyes.

"Hello?"

"Robert?"

"Yes?"

"I hope I have the right Robert Edwards. I used to work with Shelby."

There was silence on the other line. In fear that he may hang up Mayla spoke, "Robert, I did not call to harass you. I need your help."

"Help? For what?"

"I need to see you."

"Why?" he asked.

"Please Robert. It has to do with Shelby."

"I really don't see any reason why we need to."

"I think I may know who murdered her." Mayla interrupted.

"When would you like to meet?" He did not hesitate to ask.

"Now. I need to see you now. I need to meet you somewhere private, that I can't be seen."

"I can come to your home."

"No. I don't want anyone to see you coming in here. May I come to your home?"

"You may come to my mother's home."

"I know its past nine, but it's urgent."

"Very well."

Robert gave Mayla the address and directions. She arrived in less than twenty minutes after she hung up.

Robert's mother Constance Edwards opened the front door.

"*Stunning woman.*" She thought. "Hello. I'm here to see Robert."

"Follow me." She was polite.

Her home was beautiful decorated. Eclectic in a way. Original art pieces hung from the wall. Mayla was escorted to the den in the back of the house.

"May I get you something to drink?" Constance asked.

"No thank you." She saw Robert stand from a leather chair as she walked in.

Extending his hand, "Hello. I'm Robert Edwards. I've heard quite a bit about you."

Mayla smiled, "It's nice to meet you too. Finally. I've seen you before."

"I was at the funeral. In the back."

"I see."

"How can I help you?"

"I'm sorry to call and bother you Robert, but I need your help. I know you didn't murder her, But I have a feeling I may know who did."

"Who? Why? Why would anyone want to harm her?"

"You broke her heart." Mayla felt the need to give him a poke.

"Yes, I suppose I did." Robert looked into his glass of iced tea.

"I'm sorry. I didn't come here to make you feel bad." Mayla felt guilty.

"I was falling in love with her. I jumped the gun. I should have waited to pursue her. If I would have been patient, in another month my house in Boca would have been finished."

"So you really were in love? You wanted to be with her? You didn't just want her for a mistress?"

"Never. She excited me so much I couldn't wait to see her. So I did whenever I could." He paused, "I stayed with my wife, Neddie. We thought it would be all right. We were getting a divorce because we had fallen out of love with each other, but we still respected and cared for one another. I should have moved out just as soon as we decided to get a divorce but it was too convenient to stay. I moved into another room. I met Shelby a month too early."

Sadness appeared on his face. Mayla remained somber. She mistook Robert for a bad man.

"We all cared so much for her Robert."

"If you need me to help you find out who did this horrible thing to Shelby, I will. Just tell me what you need."

"First I must explain what is happening at the firm I work for."

"Go on."

"Tomorrow, my boss and I are going to trial on the Riley case."

"I've heard of it." He said.

"Well, as you know it was an insurance scam. Mr. Riley, who is the underwriter, took out life insurance policies on people who were half dead. He had forged medical documents, addresses and phony next of kin's so he can take payment for the policy when the insured dies."

"I understand." Robert said, "Did the family of the deceased know of this?"

"No. The insurance company had gotten suspicious and did an investigation because two policies were taken out on the same person. That and he tried to open an account at a bank that a deceased person used to bank at."

Robert leaned back in his chair and nodded as Mayla continued to speak.

"Mr. Riley claims the money he embezzled from the insurance companies was sent to Cuba. He said he has no record of the money he sent over. He claims that his wife's brother was assassinated by Castro's clan for trying to escape Cuba. His wife is now numb to the world around her. His death was very hard on her. Though far away, they were apparently very close."

"How do you expect to win that one?"

"Total sympathy."

"What does this have to do with Shelby?"

"Well, I thought nothing until today. Before Shelby left to go to London with you, she had been instructed by Michael, her boss and partner at the firm to deliver a white envelope. She forgot. I guess she was excited to be going away with you."

That comment made Robert smile. Mayla continued to talk.

"She called me and asked me to do it. I forgot. I had gotten so involved with the chocolates she had in her desk that I made a mess of my blouse, placed the envelope on my desk and went to the restroom to clean it. I've had so much going on, first the hurricane, and then Shelby, the Riley case, a trip to New York with a man I fear may be involved. I don't know."

"Who's the man?"

"My boss, another partner at the firm his name is Tom Wheeler. Until this afternoon I thought I might be falling for him."

Robert nodded as he listened intently; "I found the envelope today. It took me all day to find you."

"What's in the envelope Mayla?" Robert asked.

"I believe its part of an insurance scam. I found the same papers that Mr. Riley used in his scam. Shelby was instructed to deliver these per Michael. I know she had done it several times before."

"Where was she to deliver this envelope to?"

"Just a mailbox place on Federal Highway in Ft. Lauderdale. I have the exact address in the office."

"It sounds like you may be right Mayla. Thank you for coming to me. Maybe Shelby was involved too, but how?"

"I would guess the only way she was involved was by delivering these envelopes for Michael. I'm afraid I may be responsible for her death. I don't think she was taking part in the scam, it's just not like Shelby."

"I tell you what I can do. I will call my private investigator and have him work on this for me. What I need from you is that address. I'll need the make and model of Michael's car and a photograph of him. Any information on him that you can get give it to me."

"How many partners are in the firm?"

"Three."

"So there is Michael, who was Shelby's boss, and Tom, your boss."

"Yes. Then there is Max. He came to Michael after law school wanting to start a firm down here. From what I've been told, Max is the money behind the firm. I fear Tom, the gentleman that has taken an interest in me, is involved because he and Michael are very close friends. They went to law school together."

"I'll get started on this right away."

"How will I be able to work?"

"You will have to do the best you can. I will find out about your friend Tom so we can alleviate that stress and decide whether or not we need inform him of what his partner is doing. Meanwhile, since you know about the scam, you are involved. You cannot leave your job or the firm. Just continue your relationships at work as you normally would. You will have to work on the Riley case best you can. If you are able, I would like the name of Mrs. Riley's brother and if you have his last known address in Cuba that would be helpful. Don't speak to anyone else about this."

"I'll get you anything I can. I will contact you tomorrow with more information."

Robert wrote down his cell phone and work numbers on a yellow post it note and handed it to Mayla as she stood up.

"Thank you again Robert, and I'm sorry if I bothered you."

"You weren't a bother Mayla. I want to help you. I'm glad you came to me with this."

As she stood by the door to the den she turned to ask him a burning question.

"So you did love her didn't you."

"Very much so."

He walked her to the front door. Constance was sipping tea in the kitchen. They shook hands.

"Good night." Robert opened the front door.

"Night."

CHAPTER TWENTY-FIVE

"Good Morning." It was Tom who came to Mayla's office handing her a coffee from Starbucks. "Are you ready for our big day? You certainly are dressed for it."

"Thank you and yes I am." She replied as she turned to look at him and take the coffee he was handing her.

"Thanks."

"Max will be flying down to watch us in action. He seems to have taken a special interest in this case, not to mention the publicity. I think he wants to be on television."

"I'm sure he will. I'm surprised the government didn't get a hold of this case with the story we're using. Instead, he could be going to jail for attempted murder on Castro."

"Innocent until proven guilty." Tom said.

"When do we need to be there?" Mayla asked.

"Nine."

"We better get moving then." Mayla hadn't looked at Tom since he first set foot in her office. Usually, in the morning she would go to his office.

"Something wrong with you?"

"No. Why do you say that?" She sipped her coffee.

"You are not yourself. A little too business like."

"Just prepping myself."

"I see." Tom said, "Just make sure you are sitting near the front. I need your support."

"Support you shall have."

Mayla stood to grab her attaché' case and purse.

"Let's go."

"I'll drive." Tom said.

Everyone sent well wishes as they exited the firm.

"I'll see you two later when Max arrives. Looking good Tom." Michael said standing by the front door.

"Thanks."

Mayla reached work an hour early that morning to gather information from the Riley case to give to Robert. That afternoon, after the opening arguments the court took a short recess where Mayla was able to contact Robert giving him the last know address of Mrs. Riley's brother in Cuba. She also gave him names of banks, addresses of the deceased insured. When the court returned to session Mayla became very nervous. She sat next to Michael and Max in the courtroom. Unable to have eye contact with Michael and Max, knowing the two were somehow involved with this case. She claimed to have indigestion. Max offered her an antacid.

"Thank you." She whispered.

Much of the evidence that day was presented to the jury. No one had taken the stand in Mr. Riley's defense. His wife did not show up nor did any of his children. He sat alone next to Tom.

Later that evening, Max, Tom and Michael would have dinner at a pub not far from the place where they used to go for happy hour. It would give Mayla a chance to contact Robert.

"Robert? Hi it's Mayla." She was on her way home from court.

"Hi Mayla. Can you meet me for dinner?" he asked.

"I'd rather not."

"I'm sorry. I have forgotten you do not want to be seen with me. Come to my mother's again. We can have dinner there."

"Fine. I'll be there at seven."

She arrived promptly with notes from the trial that day.

"Hello Mayla." Constance opened the front door; "Robert is expecting you. I'm going to go shopping. My good son told me if I'd get lost, he would by me a new blouse. So I am!"

"Thank you." Mayla said Constance closed the door on her way outside. Robert stood waiting.

"Hello." Robert greeted her, "Please, come this way. I hope you don't mind, but I've ordered Chinese, thought we could get some things done."

Mayla followed Robert to the kitchen. There was a gentleman sitting at the round kitchen table.

"I would like you to meet someone." Robert said.

Mayla shook her head, "I don't think you understand Robert. I don't want anyone to know I'm here."

"This is my private detective that I hired. He found the Jamaican man and was able to free me of any murder charges."

"Yes, I didn't." she hesitated.

"My name is Randy Hunter." He extended his hand to shake hers. "Don't' worry Mayla, your secret is safe with me. Mr. Edwards pays me to keep quiet."

She smiled, "I just don't want,"

"I understand. You don't want to be the one to have blown the whistle."

"That's right."

Randy Hunter was a simple man. Tall with strong facial features and a well kept body. He wore a pair a Levi's and a golf shirt from a country club in Minnesota.

"I thought it was too cold to play golf in Minnesota."

"There's always that one day a year."

She sat down in-between the two men. A little intimidated, she almost felt as if they were ganging up on her. Randy was constantly reassuring her that no one will find out what she is up to.

"I need to know if Tom is involved also."

"I don't think he is." Detective Hunter said. "I was there today. In the courthouse. He seemed to pretty passionate about his work."

"You were there today?"

"Yes I was. I was watching you also, you need to relax."

"I can't."

"Practice then. Max seems to be a pretty intuitive character."

"I know he is." She said, "thank you for ordering dinner Robert."

"Your very welcome." Robert replied.

"I need to know about Tom." She began to pry.

"Let me tell you why I do not believe Tom is involved." Randy Hunter seemed reassuring.

Mayla felt a tinge of relief.

"How? Why?" She asked.

"I have a hunch."

"Mayla," Robert said, "I have given the contents of the envelope to Randy."

"And?" she looked to Randy.

"I have done some research on the papers, it's seem they have stopped processing the policies. My guess is because they lost track of the envelope. There are no accounts at any of the banks that are on the list and I have checked on these money orders with American Express to see if anyone had claimed them to be lost or stolen, no one has. If someone else were to find the envelope they would have no idea what it was and would more that likely try to cash the money orders. The only reason why you know what it is, is for the obvious reasons. Your are working on the Riley case."

"I feel horrible blowing the whistle on my firm, but I can't help but believe this may have something to do with Shelby's death. If it doesn't, I'd like to stay out of this."

"We can arrange that." Detective Randy Hunter said.

The Chinese food arrived. Mayla could barely eat.

"Don't worry. We will find out about Tom. He hasn't given you any hints has he?"

"None. I know he's upset that he is representing Mr. Riley for free."

"Free!" Randy looked at Robert.

"Yes, something to do with Max owing Mr. Riley a favor. I guess it was his father that sent Max to law school. Apparently Max was not from a wealthy family."

"I see." Randy shook his head and raised his eyebrows as he used his chopsticks to maneuver a piece of chicken into his mouth. "I have a funny feeling."

"What?" Mayla asked.

"Not until I'm certain. Tomorrow."

"Randy why don't you tell her everything you have found out in such a short time." Robert said.

"Just that Mrs. Riley's brother Carlos was indeed killed. And he was not wrapped up in anything to do with Castro. In fact, he was a huge supporter of Castro."

"And?" She asked.

"So why would he want to oust him?" Detective Randy Hunter asked.

"Could be he just wanted to be close enough to Castro to have him assassinated."

"Doubt it. Do you have any idea how difficult that would be? It's a scam. We'll find out more tomorrow. I'll investigate Max and Tom."

"So what you have found out is that this money was not used for anything to do with Castro?"

"That's right."

"Oh god." Mayla shook her head. "Why me. I don't think I want anymore to do with this."

"Too late." Robert said. "We need you."

"Why do you need me?"

"Shelby." Robert said.

"Robert please. I feel like a rat. No one can know about this."

"They won't Mayla." Hunter said.

"Please find out what you can. I need to know if Tom is involved."

"Mayla," asked Randy, "How long has he been working on this case?"

"Quite a while. And he's pissed that Max has him working on it at no charge."

"Hmm." Randy looked over to Robert, "Interesting."

"I guess he's not too happy about that." Robert said.

"He complains about it all the time." Mayla reached for a fortune cookie.

"I'll know in the morning." Randy said.

"I'll call you tomorrow." Robert looked over towards her and touched the top of her hand.

Mayla understood why Shelby fell so hard for him. He was a very compassionate man. He had gained Mayla's trust in such a short time.

"Well I must be going. Thank you Robert. It was nice to meet you Randy."

Robert walked Mayla to the front door, "Don't worry."

Mayla drove home that night constantly checking her rear view mirror feeling afraid that someone might have followed her to Robert's house. When she arrived home Tom had called her to see if she was feeling any better. She would wait until the morning to see him.

Chapter Twenty-six

"I called you last night." Tom met Mayla in the elevator at the parking garage.

"I know. I'm sorry. I didn't get the message until this morning. You must have called me while I was in the shower."

"Is everything okay? You are acting a bit out of character for yourself."

"I think all this work is getting to me."

"When this is over, we'll do something a little on the wild side." Tom spoke looking at the numbers on the elevator.

"Okay. Bahamas?" She didn't smile. She said anything to quiet him.

"Where ever you like." He was satisfied with her answer. The elevator doors opened. They proceeded to the main elevator that took them to their office.

"Happy hour?" Tom continued to test her.

"No. Dinner at seven. A quick bite."

Satisfied again.

Julie was at the front desk reading an article on '*how to satisfy your man*' in the latest copy of Glamour. She peeped above her magazine long enough to notice other people were in the office aside from herself.

"Max and Michael are looking for you Tom. They are in the conference room."

"Thank you."

Mayla said nothing to her.

"Good morning gentlemen." Tom entered the room.

"Sit down Tom." Max said. "We need to talk about a possible guilty verdict."

"Guilty? It won't happen."

"How do you know that Tom." Max stood and began to pace around the room.

"This is South Florida. Cubans everywhere. The melting pot of the new millennium. No way. He will do time. But he won't die there." Tom was confident.

"We'll see then." Max said. "I just need you to do your best work. You know he is a personal friend of the family."

"I understand that Max. I will get him a lesser sentence."

"Will you be footing his bill too?" Tom thought. There was bitterness but Tom needed Max just as much as Max needed him. After all, it was Max who put the firm together. He had the money.

"Will you be sitting in on the trial again today?" Tom looked at Max.

"I think I will. As I said, he is a friend of the family. Besides, I like to watch you work Tom. Very entertaining."

"Thanks. Anything else?"

"No."

"I need to get to work then."

Tom left the conference room and went directly to Mayla's office. "We should go."

"So soon?"

"Lets get some coffee. Starbucks." Tom seemed annoyed.

"Okay."

"Why is everyone acting so strange?"

"What do you mean?" Mayla questioned.

"First you seem to be avoiding me, then Max and Michael call me into the conference room for what I thought to be an important meeting, and it turns out they were questioning my ability to defend this guy."

"Well Tom, I'm sorry. I can only speak for myself."

"He must not know anything."

There was silence.

"Well are you going to speak for yourself?" Tom opened the passenger door to his car.

"Yes." She answered.

Tom walked to his side of the car and let himself in.

"I'm listening."

"Honestly Tom," She said, "I've never, I'm afraid of."

"Don't be." He held his hand to her face. "I enjoy your company. I enjoy you. We have a great time together. I would be happy just to hang out with you. To have your, ah, you know, would be icing on the cake. But to hang with you is enough for me."

Mayla nodded. *This is not who I thought him always to be.*

Mayla felt strange sitting in the courtroom watching Tom defend Mr. Riley based on his story of Cuban rafters knowing it wasn't true. She wanted to stand and tell the truth. Mid morning she turned to see a familiar face walk into the courtroom. It was Randy. He was wearing jeans with an old tweed jacket. He had big hair for a man. Very late nineteen eighties. His face was unshaven. He made no eye contact with Mayla. No one in the courtroom recognized him or even acknowledged that he was there.

Luciana Hernandez was on the stand. She spent several days in the hospital after her float to freedom at the age of fourteen. She was telling her story. Her brother lost his life at age sixteen. She was left to fend off the sharks by herself alone at night, in the rain until boaters heading for the Bahamas spotted her. The jury seemed interested and sympathetic. It was working.

The prosecution seemed annoyed at the bravery of Tom Wheeler's defense. When they weren't objecting to Luciana Hernandez's testimony they sat with their heads in their hands. Shaking it in disbelief.

"Objection your honor, this has nothing to do with the case."

"Over ruled, you may proceed."

Tom was getting sympathy from the judge.

Mayla turned again to glance at the man in the tweed coat. He winked. Pretending not to see him, she quickly turned her head. She did not want Michael or Max to notice him.

"I think we can start closing arguments by tomorrow." Michael whispered to Mayla as he leaned into her right ear, "look at how pathetic the jury is."

She felt like standing and telling the jury it was all a lie. She couldn't. Not yet.

Late that afternoon after court was let out for the day. Television new crews stood outside the doors to the courthouse on Andrews Avenue and Sixth Street. They had their satellite dishes propped up as they waited for Tom Wheeler, the defense attorney to immerge from the building. When he did, they swarmed like a group of crazed teenagers after Elvis.

"Mr. Wheeler!" It was a petite blond pushing her way to the front. "How are things looking for Mr. Riley right now?"

"Mr. Wheeler!" A tall geeky man with a lisp "How is Mrs. Riley?"

"Mr. Wheeler!" Reporters were shouting his name from every direction. Max and Michael stood in the background; "This calls for a celebration." Max said.

"I have a scotch so smooth you will mistake for butter." Michael said.

"We'll meet Tom at the office."

Mayla returned to the office to check her voice mail and return some calls before she went home to get ready for dinner. There were no calls from Robert or Randy the private investigator. She checked her cell phone and there were two messages.

"Mayla, Randy. Please return my call."

"Mayla it's Mom, I've been worried about you. Please call me."

She sat at her desk arranging papers for the next morning.

"Hey." It was Tom poking an eye into her office.

"Hey is for horses."

"Did you see all the publicity?"

"I sure did." She tried to sound excited. *Remember Mayla, you know nothing. Be exited for him. He may not be involved.*

"You are going to be a star here soon!"

"Come have a drink with us."

"I thought we were having dinner."

"We are. Just a quick drink in Michael's office sort of a mid-week happy hour."

You know nothing. Have a drink.

"Okay." She stood and followed Tom.

"Mayla!" You have worked so hard we'd like to make a toast to you also!" It was Max.

She smiled and gracefully accepted her snifter.

"Thank you. It looks like we will be expanding."

"We hope so. Hell even if the jury doesn't buy our defense, think of all the free advertising we've been receiving."

Mayla turned to Tom and showed him her white teeth, "Looks like I'll be getting a raise." She took a small sip of her scotch. It was nice as it warmed her insides. Max and Michael watched her.

"Would you care to join us for dinner tonight Tom?" Asked Max. Mayla couldn't wait to hear his response. "We'll be going to the Tower Club."

"An invitation I hate to turn down gentlemen, as I have a prior commitment."

Just what Mayla wanted to hear, he turned down an invitation to the exclusive Tower Club where you have to be a member in order to dine there.

Michael glanced at Mayla, "I understand Tom. Well, I am going to invite my wife."

"Great idea." Max said, "Mayla, care to join us."

"I too have a previous engagement." She never looked at Tom when she spoke.

"Your company will be missed."

"And on that note, it is time for me to depart. Gentleman, have a lovely evening. Tom, congratulations. Maybe." Mayla turned to leave the room.

As she reached the door she heard curse words fly from Michael's mouth, "Damn it!"

She turned to see what happened. Michael's glass had slipped from his hand and as he tried to catch it, it broke. He had a small cut on his hand and was bleeding.

"My favorite Waterford. I bought these in celebration of the opening of our office."

"Never mind the opening of the office Michael. You're bleeding." Mayla said as she reached for his hand to see his cut, "Oh that's nothing. There's a bandage in the kitchen. Come with me. We need to clean the wound." She sounded like Florence Nightingale.

Mayla bandaged Michael's hand before she left. "Next time be more careful. You may want to get a tetnus shot," Tossing the alcohol swipes in the trash, "If I have time, I will see if I can replace that snifter for you." She left the office.

"Are Tom and Mayla?" Questioned Max.

"I think so. Or they are at least testing the waters."

"A handsome couple. Will Marlene be meeting us at the Tower Club then?"

"Yes."

"Have we ever found the envelope?" Asked Max.

"I'm afraid not Max. I've searched everywhere. If someone finds it, there will be nothing in it for him or her to connect it to us. Our name is no where on the envelope."

"I am trusting you on this one Michael."

CHAPTER TWENTY-SEVEN

"Hello?" Answered Randy the private investigator.

"Randy, it's Mayla."

"Mayla! How are you?"

"Fine." There was anxiety in her voice. "Find anything out?"

"I did. Can we meet?"

"I can't. I'm having dinner with Tom. I was told to act normal. I even had a drink with Max and Michael."

"Good."

"Michael was so excited about the way this trial is going and all the publicity we've received he broke out his two- hundred dollar bottle of scotch, and actually invited me to have a drink. It's a good thing I did. He broke the glass and I had to play nurse."

"How's that?" he asked.

"He cut his hand. I played an attentive nurse. I Cleaned him up with an alcohol swipe and bandaged him up and told him to get a tetnus shot."

"That's perfect."

"I'm a great actress." She said proudly.

"Well, I have great news. Your friend Tom has no idea what is going on so you can enjoy dinner tonight."

"Really?" Mayla was felt relief rush into her body followed by excitement, "how do you know?"

"Mr. Riley is not a friend of the family. I have a sneaking suspicion about everything. I need to meet with you, Tom and Robert to talk about this. What we are dealing with can be very dangerous."

"Dangerous? How?" Her excitement dwindled as now she was in fear of her life.

"Mayla, you need to get that alcohol swipe that you left in the office."

"Why?"

"We need Michael's blood."

"What! Are you crazy?"

"We may need it. I suggest you stop by there before dinner."

"How am I supposed to get in there? I don't have a key."

"Then take Tom. He has a key right?"

"Yes."

"You need to get the alcohol wipe. We just may have a murder suspect."

"Murder suspect? So I was right?"

"Mayla."

"Randy." She answered.

"Mayla you need to do what I am telling you. I may be wrong, but I don't want to chance blowing what I have come up with."

"What have you come up with Randy? You are scaring me."

"Mayla, please. You need to trust me and just do what I tell you."

"Have you called those two detectives that have been working on the case?"

"No, and it's best that we do not involved them. Not yet anyway."

"What will I tell Tom?"

"Be creative. I'll call you tomorrow, plan to meet around seven. Bring your friend Tom."

The line went dead.

"Oh god." Mayla said as she set her phone on the seat next to her. *What will I do if they are still there? How will I get it? Who and what am I working for? Who are these people? Who else is involved?*

Tom picked Mayla up at her condo just before seven. Mayla convinced Tom she had to stop by the office as she thought her wallet was there. She told him she could not put her mind to ease unless she had it. He took her there. She ran to her office. Not there. The restroom, not there. The kitchen. Bingo. Her wallet magically appeared as she took it from her purse placed it on the counter next to the coffeepot. With her heart beating frantically she began to dig through the garbage.

I can't believe I am here eight o'clock in the evening digging through this disgusting trash. Gross, coffee grinds up my nails. Who and the hell would eat this?

"What are you doing?"

Mayla popped her head out of the trash. It was Tom.

Pretending she did not see her wallet, "Well you never know. It wouldn't be the first time I would threw something of value away."

She spotted the alcohol swipe. Tom spotted her wallet.

Go away! I have to get this!

"It's here." He reached for it and handed it to her.

"Oh! Thanks my hero." *Shit. Now what do I do?* "Are we ready to go?"

"I only came here for you." Tom stood impatiently.

"Will you turn the lights off in my office while I wash my hands? Please?" She begged.

Tom didn't say a word as he left the kitchen to her office. Mayla carefully wrapped the alcohol swipe in a paper towel while looking over her shoulder, and slipped it into a side pocket in her purse. "I can't believe I'm doing this." *I can't believe I'm working against a man I have cherished for two years.* She washed her hands and turned out the light. Relief.

"Since we're down this way we can get a burger on A1A."

"Sounds good."

They parked the car and walked to the busy oceanfront. There were many people out for a Tuesday night. The bar they had dinner at was a hole in the wall. It had great food. Conch fritters, calamari, fish bites and of course, great burgers. The floors were dirty; the tables were made of laminated wood. The chairs were mismatched and some were broken. The place as Tom would say 'had character.' They each had a hamburger and a beer.

"So," Mayla hesitated, as she had to ask him for a date tomorrow night. "Do you have any plans for tomorrow evening?"

"Why?" Tom had a way of embarrassing her.

"I'd like to see you."

"Really!" He seemed excited then crushed her ego, "I can't."

"Why?"

"Have to wash my hair." He smothered a greasy fry with a mixture of ketchup and mustard and shoveled it in his mouth.

"So would you like me to pick you up?" She bravely asked.

"Where you taking me?"

"It's a secret."

"I don't like secrets."

"Deal with it." She drank the last of her beer.

Tom's eyes opened wide, "And to think I gave up a night at the Tower Club to take this from you."

"So did I."

"I suppose you did."

They ordered another round of beers.

"Play you in darts." Tom challenged Mayla.

"Be careful."

"I wonder if this will ever go any further? Is this guy afraid to kiss me?" Mayla spoke to herself.

"She'll probably want to wait until she's married to have sex." It was Tom's turn. All night they talked to each other and to themselves.

"So what time will you pick me up?"

"I need to tell you tomorrow."

Tom thought he was in for a special treat. *Maybe she is making me dinner. Maybe it will be our first night of togetherness. Maybe under the moon after they shared a bottle of wine. I'll kiss her again, but better than I did in New York, so she won't resist me. If only I could have her once I'm sure I could get her to commit again and again. God she smells good. Should I come prepared?* He could only hope.

At night's end, Tom walked Mayla to her front door where he kissed her on her cheek and left her. She watched him part standing on her tiptoes looking at his bottom through her peephole. He stretched his arms as he disappeared.

"Nice butt." Mayla whispered.

CHAPTER TWENTY-EIGHT

The next day had drifted by slowly in the courtroom. The testimonies of Cubans were beginning to bore the jury. Tom feared he might have let them hear too much. He needed to save the story of Mrs. Riley for last. Mr. Riley's wife that he loved so dearly. Mayla studied Tom and his tactics as he defended his client that sat closely to him. His demure was charming. Powerful. She envied him. While losing his temper with the prosecution he put it aside long enough to wink at Mayla. She smiled and sunk slightly in her chair. She thought the entire courtroom had witnessed it. Michael and Max looked over to her. It was evident a romance would be taking place in the office.

That evening Mayla went to retrieve Tom at his home. She arrived early and in her purse she had the alcohol swipe safely secured.

"Hello." She stood at the front door in a red summer dress and black sandals. Her scent was light and florally.

"You look nice." Tom said.

"Thank you." She stepped in and waited for Tom turn to the lights off. "Ready?" She asked.

"Where are you taking me?" he closed the door behind him then locked it.

"I'll tell you in the car."

"I can't wait."

Mayla began to show signs of nervousness. Tom may know what is going on in the firm, but she had to trust the private investigator and Robert.

"We're having dinner at a friends house."

"So, you're not taking me back to your house for let's say a romantic dinner? Where afterwards we could have walked on the beach under the moonlit sky, holding hands? Where the stars will blush when you throw yourself at me?"

"You sound like a romance novel." Mayla cut him off, "I'm afraid not."

"Hmm. I see."

"Just be patient." She said concentrating on the road.

"Trying."

They arrive at Mrs. Edwards's home.

"Who lives here?" Tom asked as they pulled into the brick driveway.

"A friend I told you."

They walked to the door. Robert answered this time. He sent his mother out shopping again. He asked them to come in as he looked around to see if they had been followed.

"Tom." Robert shook Tom's hand.

"What are we doing here?" Tom whispered to Mayla as they followed Robert into the kitchen.

"Shh." She whispered.

There was a man sitting at the table in the kitchen. He stood to shake Tom's hand.

"My name is Randy Hunter. I'm a private investigator."

"Tom Wheeler." He extended his hand, "Nice to meet you."

Mayla smiled faintly as Tom looked over to her. He was polite. It was obvious he was uncomfortable in the home of someone who was once to have thought to have murdered a close friend of his.

"Would you like a drink Tom?" Robert asked.

"Sure. Gin and tonic."

"Mayla?"

"Yes. I'll have the same." She sat at the table next to Randy.

"I have baked ziti in the oven. My mother made it."

"So," Tom said as he sat at the table, "It has been nice to meet your Randy and Robert. Now, why am I here?" He looked towards Mayla. She did not look back.

"Mayla discovered something. She wasn't sure who to turn to so she called Robert." Randy sipped his drink.

"Mayla? Why couldn't you come to me?" Asked Tom.

"Because Robert had already been cleared for the murder of Shelby Peterson." Randy answered for her.

"I see. So you thought I was a suspect Mayla?" He was clearly upset.

"No. Yes. Maybe. But there's more. Please, just listen. You will understand Tom. Please don't be angry with me."

Robert sat at the table with them.

"Start from the beginning Mayla." Robert directed her.

"Before Shelby was to leave to go to London with a Robert, Michael had asked her to deliver an envelope. She forgot. She called me and asked me to do it. I was in your office when she called Tom. I went to her desk to find this white envelope; I also found some chocolates. They had a liquid center. When I bit into it, the liquid center all spilt all over my blouse."

"I saw you that day. I watched you. It was amusing." Tom interrupted her. She smiled so slightly.

"Anyway. I had to clean my blouse. It was new. I ran to my desk and tried to use a tissue. It wasn't coming out. I went to the restroom where I spent fifteen minutes trying to get the spot out. I completely forgot about the envelope. Files and newspaper clippings from the Riley case buried it. Then the hurricane came. Time past, I forgot. I just forgot." Mayla showed signs of tears. "It's possible that I am responsible for Shelby's death."

Tom didn't know what to say. He looked to Randy and Robert for help. He shook his head and shrugged his shoulders.

Randy looked at Robert asking him to speak. Mayla was crying. "The papers contained information that if in anyone else's hands they would not know what it was, but Mayla knew because of the Riley case."

"I don't understand." Tom was becoming frustrated. His romantic evening was turning out to be anything but.

"I believe Michael is involved with this Riley case. I think he is one of the so called ring leaders." Mayla stopped crying enough to speak again. "Do you have the envelope Robert?" He handed it to her. "See?" She said as she handed it to Tom. Look at these papers. We know what they are because we are working on this case. It's just names and money orders. It's the same thing Mr. Riley did except now that he's at trial they have moved on to someone else. Except we don't know who."

Tom examined the papers. He shook his head in disbelief. "So if there is another person, there is no story about Cuba, is there?"

Randy shook his head no. Tom stood. "I don't get it. You mean to tell me Michael has known about this all along?"

Mayla shook her head yes.

"What about Mrs. Riley's brother? He was murdered by Castro's people."

Again Randy shook his head no. "No Tom. He was murdered, but not by Castro's clan. He was a huge supporter of Castro."

"How do you know?"

"I'm a private investigator. That's how I know. He was killed on the streets of Cuba. No one knows by whom. Castro was at his funeral. I read it in the papers. Also, Mrs. Riley did in fact try to kill herself but not because of story of Castro murdering her brother, but because she knew the truth about her husband and whom he was involved with. Mrs. Riley tried to kill herself because she wanted nothing to do with this insurance scam. She is a strict Catholic woman."

"We should have done more research Tom." Mayla was desperate.

"We shouldn't have taken his word." Tom was beginning to get angry. "I'm trying this guy for free. By orders of Max. Max said Mr. Riley's father put him through college. He said he owed the Riley family. Now I suppose your going to tell me different."

"I am." Randy said. "Mayla had told me, so I had investigated Max Simoni's family history. He is, and always has been a very wealthy man. His family has always owned a string a businesses since the late eighteen hundreds."

Mayla sat up straight. She had not heard this yet.

"There's much more."

Tom began to pace. "How can there be much more? How can it get any worse?"

"It can." Randy assured. "The Simoni family is, they are," he paused, "They are New York."

"You mean Mafia." Tom stated.

"That's what I mean."

"Ah shit. I'm involved with the Mafia?"

"Didn't Max fund you and Michael to start the firm?"

"Yes, but."

"He wanted to start a new scam. Here in sunny South Florida. Insurance. The perfect scam! There's old people everywhere, just dropping like flies. He thought he could find a couple of unsuspecting, fresh out of law school guys. You two were perfect. Michael is the weak one, and you are the smart one. Michael was happy where he was at, but it was very easy for Max Simoni to convince him that he should have a nice office on Las Olas. It was easy for you to be convinced also. You crave nice things."

"So now I know my office is run by the Mafia and I am defending a guy who is probably afraid of them so he made up this Cuban story?"

"That's right."

"This is crazy. This sounds like a movie. My career is going to be destroyed!" He stood and began pacing.

"There's more Tom." Mayla looked over at him. He was angry.

"I really wish we were on the beach Mayla. What else do you need to tell me?"

"Tom." Mayla spoke, "The reason we went back to the office the other night was to get the alcohol swipe with Michael's blood on it."

"Why?" He asked.

"He may have murdered Shelby." Randy said

"He would never!"

"If not Michael, chances are it was one of Simoni's men." Randy said. Robert stood by sipping his cocktail occasionally checking the ziti.

"Why would he get involved with something like this?"

"Money. He has a wife and two daughters. He is not very strong man, Tom. You are. That's why Max chose him. That's why I think he may have killed Shelby. I saw him in that courtroom. He's Max's little puppet."

"Boy, you really check up on people don't you?"

"I do. You want me to tell you what color your underwear are?"

Tom found no humor in the statement Randy made. Mayla gave the alcohol swipe to Randy.

"Here it is." She wasn't proud of her find.

"I'll have it tested. Hopefully we'll know something tomorrow. I have a few friends at BSO; they should be able to help me out. They'll test this, and compare it to what was left under Shelby's nails."

"Why don't we call the police?" Tom asked Randy.

"No. We need to have the facts straight. Then we need to make sure you two will be safe. We can't let them know it was Mayla that figured this mess out."

"So I continue fibbing through the trial."

"A little while."

Randy was the only one who ate his pasta.

"I wish I would have never found that envelope." Mayla said to Tom, "I'm sorry. I'm so sorry. If I would have delivered it, Shelby would still be alive."

"Mayla don't."

"It's true Tom."

He drove them home. "It's not your fault. But why didn't you come to me sooner?"

"I told you. I thought you were involved too."

"You should know me better than that."

"I thought I knew Michael better than that too." She began to cry again. "I can't keep acting."

"Hey, hey. Maybe you shouldn't come in the office tomorrow."

"Oh no. I have to, and so do you. You have to continue with this trial. You have to continue charming the jury." She reached for a napkin in the glove box. "Will you spend the night at my house tonight Tom? I don't want to be alone."

"I will get my car and my clothes. I will follow you home. Thank you for telling me."

She leaned on his shoulder. She felt safe there.

They arrived at Mayla's home just after eleven.

"I need a glass of wine to put me to sleep Tom. Would you like one?"

"Yes. I will get it."

Mayla went to her room to change. She returned in her blue cotton pajamas.

"Will you sleep in my room with me tonight?" She asked.

"Sure." Tom handed her the wine. He knew she wasn't making a pass at him. She wanted to feel safe and with him, she did. They drank their wine on the deck. The beach is dark and windy. They spoke few words to each other as they watched the city lights reflect on the waves that crashed into shore.

Tom was having a difficult time digesting what he had learned about his best friend today. He was remaining strong for Mayla and she sensed it.

"Tom, if you would like to talk about."

"I'm alright Mayla. I'm disappointed. Very disappointed. I just don't understand how he could buy into something like that. I knew sooner or later we would make it and have our firm on Las Olas or some other prestigious part of town. I could have waited if it meant getting involved with the Mafia. My career could be finished. Think of what will happen when the media gets a hold of this one."

She said nothing but stroked his upper back.

"I hope Michael didn't,"

"Me too."

"I never liked Max. I'm sorry Shelby is gone but I pray it wasn't Michael, that."

"I know." Mayla turned towards Tom, "I'm sorry for acting so indifferent the last couple days but I didn't know."

"I understand." He put his arm around and snuggled her under his head.

"I feel safe with you."

"I'm glad."

"Don't worry Tom. What ever comes out of this, I will do my best to help you rebuild your clientele."

"I don't know Mayla, with the negative publicity I'm going to receive, who knows what will happen."

"Don't say that Tom. You did nothing wrong." She drank the last bit of wine in her glass. "I'm sleepy. I'm so relieved you're not part of them."

She could *trust* him.

"Ready for bed?" Tom asked her.

"Yes."

Mayla went to her room first. She brushed her teeth, washed her face and crawled under the covers. Tom followed after he rinsed out the wineglasses.

She fell asleep in his arms. He held her tightly, as he could not sleep all night. She would grind her teeth.

CHAPTER TWENTY-NINE

Tom did not stop in Michael's office the next morning. He fetched his papers for court and left the office, toting Mayla along with him.

"You can't ignore him." Mayla said in the elevator. "He will know something is wrong with you."

"I can't look at the weak bastard! We have been friends for eight years! Eight damn years!" Tom was finally beginning to express his anger, "How could he sell me out like that?"

"I don't get it either Tom. We can't do anything until we know all the facts."

"And then what?" Mayla turned to Tom, "Are we going to face the Mafia by ourselves?"

"If it's necessary."

"Are you crazy? If I would have know what a mess I've uncovered, I would have left it alone."

The doors to the lower lobby opened. Max was standing there. He had a stern look on his face.

"Good morning Tom, Mayla. Heading to court?"

"Yes we are." Tom said. "Have a good morning."

"Good morning Max." Mayla smiled trying to cover Tom's behavior. Max went up in the elevator.

"Let's walk today. It's only over the bridge. It's a nice day."

Mayla did not decline.

"Really Tom, I don't know what you are planning. But if they are the ones that killed Shelby, they'll come after us. Probably when we're sleeping. Would you please quit walking so fast?"

"I'm sorry. Maybe with the help of Randy and Robert we can plan something where it won't endanger anyone."

They arrived at the courthouse.

Max walked into Michael's office.

"We have a little problem, someone is snooping around." He walked towards the window, "I don't like it Michael."

"Who could possibly be snooping Max?"

"Are you certain that no one in this firm doesn't know a thing? How close were Shelby and Mayla?"

"They had lunch together quite often and went to happy hour after work on Friday nights but that's about it."

"I see." Max said.

"How about Tom? Could it be possible that Paul Riley told him the truth?"

"Absolutely not." Michael said firmly, "Don't you think after what happened to Mrs. Riley's brother he'd keep his mouth shut? Never. He wouldn't do that to his family. And Tom would come to me. I've known him for eight years."

Max paced the floors. "Michael, you know what will happen if this gets out. If Shelby and Mayla were close, there is a good possibility that she may know something."

"We don't even know that Shelby knew anything Max. Relax! Don't get so worked up over something you know nothing about!" Michael was beginning to get angry.

"We just need to be certain. Philip."

"Philipo, Philipo, fucking Philipo! I am up to my eyeballs with Philipo!" Michael stood, "Call him! Please! Use my phone, but touch my fucking family and I'll kill you myself."

Max stopped pacing and calmly turned, "Michael sit down and don't get yourself so worked up." Max looked out the window down at the people on the sidewalk, "If you haven't a thing to hide, we mustn't worry. Now we must hurry, court is in session."

They left to watch the trial. They drove.

Michael and Max found Mayla and sat next to her. Max nodded at Tom as he turned to acknowledge them. He did nothing. Not a smile or nod back. Max sensed his anger.

"He knows." Max leaned into Michael.

Michael shook his head. "No. He does not. You are paranoid."

Court broke for recess. Max, Michael and Mayla waited for Tom to gather his papers.

"Lunch?" asked Max.

"Sure." Tom said as he ignored his eye contact.

"Good. We'll take Michael's car."

Mayla quietly followed behind. The car ride was short. They wen to an Italian restaurant on Seventeenth-Street Causeway. They were seated immediately.

Tom spread his napkin across his lap; "Does anyone feel like this case is not right? I sense that Paul is holding out on us. I'm not sure what it could be. But I'm not pleased with the way I am trying this case. The jury is tired of my defense. Does anyone have any suggestions?" He looked to Max.

"Tom I believe you are doing a stupendous job. You've practically had the jury in tears. Paul will do little time. He may lose his house, but it is a small price to pay for freedom."

"Would you like me to buy him a house too Max?" Tom stuffed his mouth with a piece of bread.

Max did not like his comment. He sat up straight. Michael shook his head. Mayla remained quiet. It seemed eons before Tom spoke again.

"Ready to order?" He looked around the table.

"No Tom, I don't believe I am." Max was very angry. "Don't forget who funded that lovely view you have."

"Will I be debt to you for life? Did I make a deal with the devil?" He held his stare on his menu.

"You are being ungrateful."

Tom placed the menu down in front of him. "And how long must I be grateful for?"

Mayla gently nudged Tom under the table.

"Tom." Michael held his hands up as if to say what are you thinking?

He backed off momentarily.

"I'm ready to order." Tom said.

Mayla wanted to crawl under the table.

"Excuse me." Mayla stood leaving a look of disapproval for Tom. She sent a fake smile to Max and Michael.

"You've upset her Tom." Max said calmly.

"Now that I have you where there is not a woman present, who and the hell do you think you are? I have given you plenty of chances to speak to me personally about this case and all you have done is act like a puppeteer with Michael."

"He has done no such thing!" Michael spoke in Max's defense.

"This is it! Come on Max! I want to hear the story! Why am I defending this man for free? Is it because you have so graciously invested your money on two of the best defense attorneys in the state of Florida that have made you fifteen times what you have invested? If Riley is such a great friend of the family, shouldn't you be paying all of his legal fees?"

It was clear to Max and Michael that this is what has been ailing him for the past few days. Max calmed Tom by admitting he was guilty of using Michael.

"I'm terribly sorry Tom. I should have spoken to you. I had every intention of doing so when you were in New York but you had a lady with you. I wanted it to be an enjoyable weekend."

Tom had calmed himself. Mayla returned to the table. They placed their order. They lunched quietly and politely.

"I need to make a phone call before I head back into the courtroom." Tom excused himself.

He stood by the window that overlooked the Broward County Jailhouse.

"Randy, Tom here. Have any news for me?"

He paused. "I see." His body was shifting. He sighed. He shook his head. "Now what?" He placed his hand on his head. His jacket rose.

"I'll talk to you this evening." Tom closes his flip cell phone. He sighed again. He stroked his face. It reflected the look of disappointment. Disgust.

He returned to the courtroom. Michael, Max and Mayla sat waiting talking amongst themselves. She looked up to him as he past by. He did not look at her. She knew what he knew, instantly. She sat quietly during the second half of the day. The jury was bored. Max studied Tom. The day ended.

Michael had gone home to his wife and daughters. Tom and Mayla would meet with Robert Edwards and Randy Hunter again.

Mayla and Tom walked back to the office. It was hot. Tom began to sweat in his suit.

"Take off that jacket and give it to me." Mayla demanded. They stopped on top of the drawbridge on Third Avenue. Tom removed his navy blue suit jacket and handed it to Mayla. "Randy has confirmed our murderer."

"Please don't say his name." She asked. "Will you stay again tonight? Or if you prefer, I will stay with you."

"We can take turns." He said as they began to walk again.

"If you don't mind. Just until this is over."

"And then what? Do I need to pray for another hurricane? Or another?"

"No." She quickly interrupted and continued walking with his suit jacket draped over her right arm. They never went into the office; instead they went directly to the parking garage then to Mayla's home.

"Would you like to shower before we meet Randy?"

"If I may."

"I'll get you a towel."

"How about a glass of wine?"

"Anything else?" She asked.

"Well." He sung.

"Here is your towel. The wine will be waiting when you're out."

They enjoyed the wine on Mayla's balcony. There was a very warm breeze that the seagulls fluttered around. A few people walked on the beach.

"Are we ready?"

"Ready for the inevitable?" Mayla asked, "I guess so."

They left.

Tom drove. "I hope Max or one of his Guidos aren't following us."

"Do you really think they could be?"

"Mayla. He is the Mafia."

Realizing what he had said, he quickly recanted his words afraid he might upset her, "Maybe not."

Randy Hunter answered the door to the Edwards home. He searched the area to see if they had been followed.

Tonight there was no dinner waiting for them. They were to have a quick meeting with Robert Edwards and Randy Hunter. They sat in the kitchen at the table. Robert offered coffee. Mrs. Edwards had gone out of town to see one of her other children.

"Now that you know, we need to find a way to bring this out in the open where both you and Mayla are safe." Randy said to Tom.

"I have a plan." They sat around the table for an hour before they finally decided to order a pizza. By midnight, a plan had been put into place. Everything was about to unfold. Randy shook Tom's hand and assured him that he and Robert would be at the trial tomorrow morning.

The courtroom was filled with unsuspecting witnesses. It would be the fall of a very powerful man. Randy Hunter contacted the investigators, Mark Williams and Brian Henke that are working on the murder case of Shelby Peterson. He invited them to sit in on the closing arguments. They had been warned that they should be prepared to make a few arrests that day.

Tom wore his favorite navy Armani suit with a matching blue tie. He looked good.

Mayla sat next to Michael and Max once again. Her hands were shaking so badly she needed to take something to relax herself. She and Tom were about to put their lives on the line.

Robert sat with Randy Hunter several rows behind Max and Michael.

The jurors were brought in the courtroom and seated. The show was about to begin.

New crews were outside waiting for the verdict. Cameramen hung patiently outside their vans munching on hotdogs from the cart across the street. It wouldn't have been such a big case if it weren't for the Cuban story that Mr. Riley had dreamt up.

Tom stood and buttoned his Armani jacket. He cleared his throat. It echoed through the courtroom. All eyes were on him.

He began to speak, "Ladies and gentlemen of the jury. For the past few days you have heard me argue this case with."

A man stood in the back row. He was a handsome tall man wearing a blue and white golf shirt. "Your honor, I'm sorry I must interrupt."

Tom stood quietly as he allowed Robert to come forward. There was a little commotion in the courtroom. All heads turned to look at Robert.

"About two months ago, I met a lovely woman. Her name was Shelby Lynn Peterson." He looked around the room, "Yes, she is the young lady that some of you may or may not know that was murdered the day of hurricane Gunther."

Michael sat up in his seat looking towards Max who did not flinch. The jury seemed confused, "What has this got to do with anything?"

"Order!" The judge began to bang her gavel. "Please identify yourself if you are going to interrupt my courtroom."

"I'm sorry your honor. My name is Robert Edwards. It was originally thought that I may have been the murderer." He spoke slowly and began to pace as if he were doing the closing arguments, "I did not murder this lovely young woman. I only fell in love with her. I took her to London with me."

"And what relevance does that have to this case Mr. Edwards?"

Before Robert Edwards could answer, Mayla stood.

"Your honor, my name is Mayla Ann Martin, I am a legal secretary for Max, Devon and Wheeler." Mayla stood and straightened her skirt. She avoided the undesirable looks she was receiving from Max. It was evident he was uncomfortable with what she was about to reveal.

"What the hell is she doing?" Max was pissed as he nudged Michael in his side with his elbow.

"What do I have here? A circus?" The judge sat up in her chair.

"I'm sorry your honor, I must continue. Before Shelby and Robert went to London." Max continued his glare at Michael "Shelby asked me to deliver this." She held up the infamous white envelope. "It's something she had been doing for quite sometime, but she had no idea what she was delivering. At first she thought her boss Michael Devon," Mayla pointed at him as if she had met him for the first time, "Was having an affair. We were all happy to find out he was not." Michael made a nervous laugh. "What he was doing however, was forwarding information about people in nursing homes who were about to well, kick the bucket so to speak." Max crossed his arms then legs. He face was turning several shades of red. He was losing control of his composure.

"Along with money orders, several of them were payable to Cramer Home, Health and Life Insurance. There are lists of nursing homes with names of people who are in poor health, and to be honest your honor; they do not have much longer to live. Mr. Cramer himself fell victim to Max Simoni." Mayla walked to stand next to Tom.

The Judge sat up to listen to the story. Detectives Mark Williams and Brian Henke shook their heads in disbelief. They knew what they were about to hear. Robert intercepted the conversation.

"Mayla had no one to turn to. She chose me because I have already been cleared of the murder. After speaking with her, I contacted my personal private investigator, Randy Hunter."

Randy Hunter stood and looked around the room. Michael and Max sat dumb founded. *How could this have possibly happened?*

"After hearing Mayla's story I had begun to do some serious research not only of the firm, but in several firms that Max Simoni is the senior partner or prime investor. It seems his other firms have defended several other insurance cases just as what we are doing here today. The only difference is the story they had come up with. In Houston, the man had a drug problem. In Vegas the woman had a gambling problem. They all had lost their money that they had embezzled from their underwriter. And oddly enough, they had all lost a loved one very close to them. All of these people on this list that I am about to hand you had a problem, lost a loved one and their attorneys were partners with Max Simoni. Major Mobster in New York City. He is the right hand and brother of Philipo Simoni; together they run some of the largest scams throughout America. Drug smuggling, insurance fraud, underground gambling, and of course, murder." After circling the courtroom he stood next to Tom.

"I couldn't help but feel I was responsible for Shelby's murder." Mayla said, "If I would have only delivered the envelope like she had asked, Max would have never thought a thing to be wrong. He would have never suspected Shelby knew anything. And sadly enough, she didn't."

Max stood and turned towards the door. The bailiff waved his hand and motioned him to sit. He obeyed.

"Private detective Randy Hunter had discovered that Mr. Paul Riley's brother in law was not murdered by Castro." There was a hush in the courtroom; "He was murdered on the streets of Cuba by an unknown assailant. He was a good friend to Castro. Why Castro himself even attended the funeral. So for the past few days, I have been lying to you your honor, and to you the people of the jury, because I believed this man." Tom continued, "Paul Riley had become very greedy at one point, just like my partner, Michael Devon who was money hungry and weak enough that he sold his sole to the devil, Max Simoni."

"We're not finished." Mayla continued as she tried to hush the court-room. "There is still something that is unanswered." She looked to Tom for support, he nodded. "It is the death of my friend, my co-worker, and a daughter of two wonderful people, Shelby Peterson." She stopped her-self from tearing. "We were invited, Tom and I to celebrate a premature outcome in the case, that was to have a drink with Max and Michael. During our celebration, Michael cut his hand. I bandaged it. Later that evening, Randy Hunter, the private detective, instructed me to retrieve that alcohol swipe that I had tossed in the trash. I did."

More commotion in the courtroom.

"Jesus." Michael shook his head and nervously began to rock in his seat. Max was about to hyperventilate.

"Order!" The judge fiercely pounded her gavel.

"I had it sent down to the Broward County forensics." It was Randy's turn to speak. "The blood matched what was found under the nails of Shelby Peterson."

"Liar!" Michael stood and began yelling. "You son of a bitch Tom! All I have done for you! Bastard! How dare you set me up like this!" He was out of control and began to step over people to attack Tom. The bailiff and BSO detectives apprehended him. He continued to scream, "You bitch! You fucking bitch!" It was time for Mayla to receive her verbal bashing.

Max sat without a flinch. He would be taken away for questioning and later arraigned on smuggling and murder. Unbeknownst to him, his brother Philipo was already in jail.

Paul Riley received a sentence of twenty years. Possible chance of parole after ten. His wife would live with her sister in Miami. The government took the house and cars, leaving Mrs. Riley no money at all. She recovered from her depression after finally being set free from the threats of the Mafia.

Channel Seven and other stations had gotten a hold of the news before Tom and Mayla had even left the courtroom. They were swarming around them on the sidewalk as they tried to pass by. Mayla stood next to Tom holding his arm and keeping pace. Randy walked in front. Robert stayed behind. It was finally over.

Max Simoni and Michael Devon never left the courtroom. They were taken directly to the Broward County Jail where Michael was booked with murder in the first degree along with insurance fraud. His wife Marlene would discover the truth about her husband on national television. She suffered a nervous breakdown in front of her two daughters. She would be hospitalized for several weeks.

Shelby's mother and father also found out the news of who viciously murdered their daughter on national television. There was relief, yet sadness and anger. They would have to sit through a very grueling trial. Something Sandy Peterson was not looking forward to.

Max's charges were much more extensive than Michael's were, as they would stem from across the United States. Charges would include murder, insurance fraud, illegal gambling and a number of money laundering schemes. He will spend the rest of his life in prison.

CHAPTER THIRTY

Robert and Randy Hunter agreed to meet Tom and Mayla at her condo. They would celebrate with a few bottles of elaborate Mondavi Reserve.

"I don't feel much like celebrating Mayla." Tom said as he removed his jacket. "Everything I have worked so hard for is gone. We'll have to close the office. I can't afford that rent myself and pay everyone else that works there."

He was moping. He excused himself to her room where he undressed himself and took a shower. He emerged in a pair of jeans and a white cotton shirt. His feet were bare.

"*Nice toes.*" Mayla said to herself.

"Do you think we're safe?" She asked Tom, as he was towel drying his hair.

"I'm sure if anything ever happened to us, even if it looked like an accident, the first place the authorities would go is to Max and his family."

"I need a shower myself. When Robert and Randy get here, let them in. Offer them some Brie, it's in the oven. Will you slice the apples? It'll give you something to do until they arrive."

Shortly after she turned the shower on the doorbell rang. Tom opened the door without looking through the peephole.

"Come on in." A man he had never seen before pushed him inside the door. He was a tall man with broad shoulders wearing a black shirt.

"Get down!" He was yelling at Tom. "Put your hands behind your head." He hog tied Tom and left him on his belly. "Where's the bitch?"

Tom didn't answer.

"Where's the bitch?" The man kicked Tom in his side. Looking around the condo, he paused when he heard the shower running. "Perfect. I get to see your little bitch naked."

"Fuck you!" Tom yelled at the big man. For his efforts he received another kick this time, in the stomach. Tom groaned.

"Piss off."

The big man went into Mayla's room. Tom felt so helpless.

He could hear her scream. Helpless. She was totally helpless. Tom noticed the front door open slowly and close suddenly. It was Randy and Robert. Randy motioned Robert to call for the police while he would attempt to take on the big man. Mayla was awkwardly wrapped in towel and thrown to the floor next to Tom.

"I hate to tell you folks this but there was no way I was going to let you off this easy. Without Max, everything I have is gone! What's so ironic about this situation is that no one knows who I am! Have you ever seen me before you son of a bitch?"

Tom did not answer until the big man kicked him in his side. Tom screeched.

"Leave him alone you bastard!" Mayla turned on her side to yell at the man.

"As for you," He paused, "You sure are a pretty fine thing."

He ran his hand across her hair.

"Keep your hands off me you bastard!"

"Come on pretty girl. I think I should take you in the other room." The man grabbed Mayla and dragged her towards the bedroom. She was screaming and crying.

"Let me go!"

"Let her be!" Tom yelled as he wiggled trying to free himself.

"Careful there pal, I may just have to put you out right now, however," the big man paused, "I think I prefer you to listen."

The man had long unkempt hair and crooked teeth. He wore snakeskin cowboy boots that his torn jeans fell over.

"We'll turn up the volume for you."

"Leave me alone!" She spit in his face.

"That's enough!" He yelled.

She upset him. He struck her across her face and she fell next to the floor by the window.

"That'll teach you bitch!"

Before another word could be said Randy Hunter kicked down the door and pulled out his revolver.

"Drop it or you're going down." He aimed directly for the man's head.

Robert phoned the police from the hall.

"Fuck off." The man reached for his gun and Randy moved his aim and shot him in the chest. He fell to the floor on his knees holding his hand over his wound after dropping his gun by his side he fell face down. Randy untied Tom. Mayla was crying hysterically. She ran to into Tom's arms after he had been set free. As she hugged him tightly, he placed his chin on her head to comfort her.

"How many more are there?" Tom asked.

"There's more. But they're not that stupid." Randy replied.

"Get him out of here!" Mayla hid her face in Tom's chest.

"Let's get some clothes on you." Tom directed Mayla to her room. "Mayla, you can't stay here. I want you to pack some clothes. You'll bring Vermin and you can stay with me as long as you like."

The police arrived with an ambulance. The man had died on the way to the hospital. Finally, the battle was over.

CHAPTER THIRTY-ONE

Tom and Mayla hid in his house for the next few days only excepting phone calls from a few friends and family. Robert Edwards and Randy Hunter were their list.

"Hello?" Tom answered the phone.

"Tom, how are you?" It was Robert.

"Fine thanks." He scratched his messy head of hair.

"And Mayla? Is she alright?"

"She's doing okay. Her mother is here now. She didn't want to fly home because she thought it would be best to deal with everything here."

"I see. I'm glad her mother is here. Tom," he paused, "I need to see you. Do you think you could play nine holes with me this afternoon?"

"Sure. It will give the girls time to spend together."

"Weston Hills Country Club? I'll call for the tee time. Say around two."

"Perfect."

Tom hung up the phone.

"Will you girls be alright if I play nine holes this afternoon?"

Mayla nodded and her mother told him to go on and get out of the house.

"We'll go get some lunch on the beach mom."

Mayla forced herself off the couch. "I'm going to take a shower."

"Okay honey. Take your time."

Tom stood in his kitchen with the French accents.

"I like you Tom. Thank you for taking care of my daughter."

"I like you too. And it is my pleasure to take care of her, even though she is very capable of taking care of herself.

"I'm glad you can make it out here this afternoon. Sorry it's a bit warm, but I'll bet you needed to have some fun." Robert said as he teed up on the first hole. "I've got a proposition for you." He took his stance and hit the ball with his Big Bertha driver. "That I must say, sounded great. But where did it go? I have a problem with my eyesight."

"It was a good shot." Tom nudged him to the side. "What is your proposition?"

"It is a business proposition."

"I'm always for a good business proposition. I'm listening." Tom stretched with the golf club behind his neck.

"Now that Max, Devon and Wheeler no longer exist. What are you going to do?"

"To be honest, haven't thought about it. Didn't want to think about it."

"Well Tom, you need to think about it."

Tom teed up and struck at the ball.

"Shit." He shook his head as they walked to the cart.

"What about your clients? Are they coming with you?"

"I hope so. Once the feds get done snooping around the office, I might be able to get back in there and contact them. Hell, maybe I'll take some of Michael's. Bastard."

"Well that is something we can work on. My proposition is I will lend you the money you need to maintain the firm as a single partner. Keep the help you have now, and we'll get some fresh attorneys to work for you. I think we may need to broaden our horizon and consider hiring a few attorneys that understand corporate law and not criminal defense. That way, I can use them."

Tom smiled and looked to Robert as he drove the cart to Robert's ball, "What do you get?"

"What do you think?"

"A percentage."

"Very good Tom."

"How much are we talking about?"

"That depends on the expenses to keep the firm up."

"I'll have to get some numbers together for you. Are you sure you want to do this?" Tom stopped the cart near his ball.

"It's what I do for a living."

"Let me ask you something Robert."

"Sure."

"Were you in love with Shelby?"

"Absolutely."

Robert struck at his ball. He put it on the green about ten feet from the hole.

"Nice. Very nice."

A deal had been stuck on the golf course that day. Eventually, Tom would single handedly manage the firm with a little bit of help from Mayla. New partners would be brought in and the firm would become more successful than it was with Max and Michael.

"This sun feels great. It's so relaxing. It's what I needed." Mayla covered herself with sunscreen as she sat on a chair near the pool that overlooked the rocky ocean.

"Would you like another rum runner?" Tom asked Mayla as he squinted towards the sun.

"No thank you."

"You know, I never told you what a wonderful job you did in the court room the other week. I think you should go back to school and take the bar."

"You think so?"

"Yes. Yes I do."

"Thanks for taking me here Tommy. I really needed this getaway."

"I told you we would come here, after the hurricane. We're a few weeks late." Tom said.

"But here we are." She smiled.

The sun continued to beat down on their oiled bodies. Tom's hand slowly crept towards Mayla's. He wrapped his fingers around her pinky and held it tightly.

Who knew that it would be possible for her to have butterflies after knowing Tom for such a long time?

"Dinner with me tonight?" He asked.

"Buy me a dress."

"If that's what it takes."

"I'll get my surrong." She said as she faced him on his chair.

"Have I ever told you?" He asked as he placed his hand on her face.

"What's that?"

"How beautiful you are?"

"No. I don't believe you have." Her reply was quick.

He bravely held his eyes on hers before stroking the side of her cheek.

"You are so beautiful and not only on the outside, you're beautiful here too." He touched her heart, and then pulled her close to his mouth then gently pressed his lips to hers. She graciously accepted.

THE END

First Bite Waiting

Hanging from a tender stem
    round and voluptuous curves
    wanting,
    first bite

    Bitter from winter
    sweet from summer
    waiting,
    first bite

    Surrounded by others
    different colors
    craving,
    first bite

    Hands have warmed
    eyes have admired
    still waiting,
    first bite

    A stroke to a peel
    an ex-ray to core

prelude to
First bite?

Touch so smooth
mouth on skin
teasing first bite

Stem is weak

River of nectar
I surrender,
first bite

Printed in the United States
23050LVS00003B/251

9 780595 178483